Prayer Trilogy

Kimberly Gordon

Energion Publications
2011

Scripture taken from the THE KING JAMES VERSION OF THE BIBLE

Cover Design: Henry & Jody Neufeld

ISBN10: 1-893729-14-1
ISBN13: 978-1-893729-14-8
Library of Congress Control Number: 2011941178

Dedication

Thanks to all my brothers and sisters in Christ who have supported my writing over the years. God bless you!

Table of Contents

A Christmas Prayer

December 23, 1875
Eastern Colorado Territory

"Dear Lord, we need a miracle now," Helen Jenkins cried out in prayer. With head bowed and hands clasped together, she knelt before the fire in their one room cabin. "Only you can save us, God. Please, hear my prayer, have mercy on these children." The words came from her mouth as tears slid from her eyes. Helen thought of her three young ones, now asleep together in one bed. They had gone to sleep with only half-full stomachs. The food was nearly all gone, maybe one or two more meals worth left. The snow had them isolated, trapped. Even if they could have gone for help, only her husband would have been able to go. The children did not have warm coats to protect them from the cold. "Lord, I do thank you for our warm cabin. And I thank you that we are all together."

Helen heard a horse whinny out in the barn. Chad was out there now, checking on their two horses. Tomorrow, he would probably have to kill one for food.

"God, thank you for the horses that we have left. But, you know we are almost out of oats, too." New tears streamed down. Helen was overwhelmed with thoughts of doom for them all. Never in their nine years on the frontier had she and Chad been through anything so difficult. This entire year had been one disaster after another.

"God, don't forsake us out here. You said you wouldn't in Joshua, chapter one, but this year..." Helen sniffed and wiped her nose. "This year has been so awful."

Helen remembered the stillborn child she had delivered last March. That was their first heartbreak. The second was the awful storm this past summer which brought with it an enormous funnel cloud. It had destroyed most of their crops. Lastly, was the barn fire this fall. Over half their animals were lost. Helen sobbed, wiping the tears from her eyes. "Oh, God, please hear me!"

After minutes of quiet crying, Helen finished her prayer. "Amen." There was nothing more she could find to say. Helen sat quietly, staring into the fire. Chad was taking an awfully long time in the barn. She knew that he, too, must be privately dealing with their current situation. He was probably praying as well.

Helen wiped her eyes again. She heard the barn door slam closed in the wind. It was beginning to blow again, stirring up the powdered snow. She looked out the small window. The white flakes were coming down again, rather thick.

Helen reached for her only wool shawl and went to the door. Chad should come back inside before the snow blinded his way. She stepped into the doorway and called his name. He was already bracing the barn door shut. He held up the lantern and swung it back and forth gently to light his way.

"Halloo," a strange voice called out from the darkness. Chad and Helen both turned toward the sound. A lantern glowed dimly through the snow.

Chad held his lantern higher. "Halloo," the voice called again. The light came closer. Helen heard the sound of sleigh bells.

"Hello there," Chad called out. He wondered who would be out in this snow storm. Their nearest neighbor was ten miles away.

The light came closer as a minute passed. Finally, coming out of the darkness was an elderly man in his heavily laden sleigh pulled by two enormous horses, the biggest Helen had ever seen. Six pack mules, all burdened down with cargo, were tied behind the sleigh.

"Greetings, friends," the man said to them, all smiles. He was wrapped in a warm bear fur-lined coat. Thick gloves covered his hands and a gray beard sheltered his face. Snow rested lightly on his warm hat.

"Hello, sir," Chad answered. Helen was silent, wondering who he was.

"Might I take shelter with you kind folks tonight?" he asked. "I'm a God-fearin' man. No harm will come to you for it, rest assured."

Chad motioned for him to come down from the sleigh. "Of course, you are welcome, sir. We have a warm fire inside. I can help with your animals."

"Praise the Lord for you both." The man climbed down and shook Chad's hand. "The name's Gabriel, Gabriel Davidson."

"Chad Jenkins. Pleased to meet you. This is my wife, Helen."

She nodded, as did the man when he touched his hat brim.

"Helen, go back into the house. It's too cold out here for you," Chad told her. "We'll be in shortly."

As Helen walked back through the doorway, she heard the man begin to speak. "You folks sure are an answer to prayer. Never thought I would see the light of day again. Wasn't expecting to be traveling back in this storm."

The men led all the animals into the rough hewn barn. The cracks between the timbers were filled with dried mud to keep out the wind. It was a warm enough shelter for the animals. Small beds of straw were on the floor for each horse.

Gabriel continued to speak. "Although, I should have known God had a plan for me. I wanted to turn around and go back, but the Lord kept telling me to keep going. He told the horses to keep goin' too, I guess. Glad I listened to Him though, or I'd no doubt still be out there somewhere freezin'."

"Where you headed?" Chad asked.

"Just been over Fort Morgan way to find my daughter and her family. I was takin' her some supplies. It's a long story. But she wasn't there, nor her husband and my grandchildren. So I turned 'round and headed back to home. Denver, that is," he explained.

"That would explain all this cargo," Chad commented.

Gabriel unwrapped two bales of hay he had taken off one donkey. He placed them where all his animals could eat freely. He also noticed the Jenkins' thin horses. "I'd like to offer your animals some as well. I have oats, too, they can eat tomorrow."

Chad was thankful for his generosity. "They'd be pleased to have it, thank you, sir."

Once the animals were fed and all Mister Davidson's crates and barrels were safely situated inside the barn, he grabbed one large satchel before heading to the house with his host. Chad carried his lantern high, as the snow still fell diagonally on the wind.

Helen was inside the house as the stranger and her husband put the animals away for the night. She wondered who he was and why he would be out here in the middle of the plains during this wintry season. And traveling at night, too – he must surely be crazy. Crazy or not though, she wished she had something hot to offer him to drink. She doubted he had eaten either, and they had so little as it was. Still, the Lord said in Matthew twenty-five, verse forty, "Inasmuch as ye have done it unto one of the least of these my brethren, ye have done it unto me." Helen knew she must offer him their food.

The men entered, bringing a cold wind and swirls of snow into the room. Gabriel Davidson noticed the three little bodies nestled together on one of the two beds. One quilt covered them, but the room was warm from the large fire. He spotted the woman, too, standing nervously near the hearth. "Ma'am," he greeted her, removing his hat.

"Helen, this is Mister Davidson. The Lord led him to us tonight."

Helen nodded her head. Chad turned to their guest.

"Please, come in and warm yourself."

Gabriel set his large satchel and hat on the table and walked to the fire. He removed his gloves. "It feels good," he said, holding out his hands for warmth. After a moment, he shed his coat as well. "I want to thank you both for your kindness tonight. I pray the Lord will bless you for it."

"Thank you, sir," Chad responded. "Anyone would do no less for a Christian brother caught in a storm."

"I would like to think so," Gabriel answered.

"Can we offer you some boiled oats, sir?" Helen asked. "Or some water?"

"Thank you kindly, but I've food in my satchel. May I offer to share some with you though?"

Helen's eyes bulged. She wondered what kind of food he had.

Gabriel opened the flap. He pulled out a sack. "Coffee, ma'am." Chad and Helen both smiled. They'd not had coffee in months. He pulled out a second bag. "Beef jerky," he told them. "There are some biscuits in here somewhere, too, but I'm afraid they're frozen right now."

"I can put them near the fire for you. I'll start water for the coffee, too," Helen offered. This man was heaven sent for certain. The children would all get a good meal in the morning. What a wonderful Christmas gift from above. God had heard her prayer!

"I'd be most obliged, ma'am."

"We only have the two beds, Mister Davidson, but we can make you a nice pallet on the floor by the fire," Chad told their guest.

"If it's all the same to you, I can just put my coat on the floor in front of it. It'll make a decent bed for me. I'll be warm as a bear," he said with a smile.

Chad and Helen both grinned. The bear fur coat surely must be warm. Helen thought of her own meager wool shawl.

"Mama, Papa?" a tiny voice called out.

Chad walked over to the bed. Little eight-year-old Naomi wiped her eyes. She looked about the room and stared at the stranger.

"Don't fret, Naomi," her father called out. "We've a guest tonight. Mister Davidson. He was caught in the storm and God led him here so we could give him shelter in our warm house."

The little girl gave Gabriel a tiny smile. Then she looked at her mother. "I'm hungry, Mama."

Helen bit her lip. She looked at the biscuits now sitting in a frying pan warming over embers. There were a dozen.

"Mister Davidson has brought us some jerked beef and some biscuits. How does that sound?" Chad asked.

Naomi nodded and crawled out of bed. Gabriel noticed the tattered state of her gown. It looked a size too small. His heart tugged inside his chest. This girl was close in age to his own granddaughter. "How old are you, young one?" he asked.

"Eight, sir."

"I have a granddaughter who is nine. Her name is Betsy. I have two grandsons, too. They are fourteen and six," he told her.

"I have two little brothers," Naomi responded. "Michael is five, Johnathan is three."

Gabriel smiled at her. "Those are very good names."

Naomi looked hungrily at the biscuits, then at their guest. "Those sure do look good. We haven't had biscuits in so long. We'll have to eat 'em plain though. We don't have no jam or honey to put on them."

Gabriel's brows furrowed. He looked at the parents. Chad's face was grim. Helen turned hers in shame. Gabriel began to wonder if God's real reason for sending him here was not to save him from the storm, but to save this poor family from starvation. Psalm seventy-two came to his mind, verse twelve and thirteen, "For he shall deliver the needy when he crieth; the poor also, and him that hath no helper. He shall spare the poor and needy, and shall save the souls of the needy."

"Well, you know what? I like my biscuits plain just fine. But tomorrow, when there's light and it's safe to go out to the barn, I'll see if I have any jam or honey out there for you."

Naomi's face lit up.

"Whatcha doin'?" another little voice called from the bed. Michael and Johnathan were both sitting up.

"Want a biscuit?" Naomi asked them with a smile.

Both boys crawled out of bed. Their father introduced their guest again.

"Hello, boys," Gabriel said to them.

Little Johnathan clung to his mother's skirt as she prepared the coffee. "Are you Santa Claus?" Michael wondered out loud.

The adults chuckled. "No, son, but I know I look like him," Gabriel answered, stroking his short gray beard. "And I do have a sleigh full of goods. But no, I'm not Santa Claus. I was sent by God."

The boys' eyes widened in awe. "Can I see the sleigh?" Michael asked.

"Yes, in the morning," their guest answered.

Both boys grinned with excitement.

"But first young men, we must say grace, because I think the biscuits are ready," Chad broke in. They all lowered their heads. "Blessed Lord, we thank you for leading Mister Davidson to our home. We thank you that we could shelter him and we thank you for his kindness in sharing his food. We ask for your blessings on this meal, Amen."

"Amen," the group echoed.

The beef jerky was passed out to everyone. Helen served water to the children, black coffee to the adults. The newly warmed biscuits were placed on the table for all to enjoy.

"We can have two each," Naomi announced, proud of her math skills.

"We sure can," Gabriel encouraged. "How did you get to be so smart?"

Naomi beamed. "Mama and Papa teach me when they have time."

Gabriel looked to the parents, then back at Naomi. "You must be very pleased to have such a smart mama and papa." The little girl nodded. "Tell me, do you ever go to school?"

Naomi shook her head. "No school to go to."

"No school to go to, sir," her father corrected.

"Sir," she added.

"Our nearest neighbor is ten miles away by Hoyt along the Bijou Creek," Chad explained. "The nearest school is even farther."

"Well then, I see your problem. Coming from a busy city, it's hard for me to imagine being so isolated," their guest commented.

"Where is it you're from?" Helen asked, her first biscuit already gone.

"Denver, Misses Jenkins. I own a store there."

"My, what brings you out so far in winter?" she inquired.

Gabriel grimaced. "It's a long story, but I guess we have all night."

Chad rose to put more wood on the fire while their guest began his story.

" 'Bout ten days ago I received a letter from my grandson, Luke. He's the fourteen-year-old. The letter was dated December first. He asked me to come for a visit this Christmastime. He told me how cold and hungry they all were and that his mother, who's my daughter, was too ashamed to write to me for help. You see, she married without my consent to an unbeliever. She's been vexed ever since with his drinking, swearing and occasional gambling. He can't seem to settle in one spot and stay there long enough to make ends meet. The children have suffered so, it breaks a grandfather's heart. I've done what I could over the years, when I knew where they were. Any way, I left the store in the hands of a friend and packed my sleigh with things for my daughter and her family. I journeyed four days, but when I got to the town where the letter had been sent from, they were already gone. No one had seen them for a week. The little old cabin they had lived in for a short time was vacant yet again, with no trace or clue as to where they'd gone. I can only assume Roger found out about the letter or heard of some poker game or something and pulled up stakes before I could arrive." Gabriel stared dreamily into the fire. "I really would have liked to have seen my grandchildren." The room was quiet. "Missy is my only child. I became a widower years ago. She and the children are all I have left."

The Jenkins family continued to listen with interest.

"I've offered to let them live with me, but Missy and Roger refuse. I know my grandchildren would be willing, but they don't have much say in things. I pray for them all every day." He was quiet again.

"We can add them to our prayers as well," Chad offered.

"I appreciate that, son," the older man replied. Helen smiled at him, her eyes filled with compassion. "So I was on my way back to Denver when the storm hit. I got off course and lost my way. And now, I'm here, thanks to the Lord."

"May God bless you and protect your daughter and her family, wherever they are," Helen told him with compassion.

"Thank you," he answered, appreciation in his smile.

Naomi got off her stool and stood next to Gabriel. "We can be your grandchildren for now if you want us to. We don't have no grandparents," she told him with a pure and earnest heart.

Gabriel was choked up. He reached out to hug her. "Thank you, young one. I'd like that."

"Me, too!" Michael called from his seat.

"Me, too!" little Johnathan added, not wanting to be left out from things.

"I am truly blessed," Gabriel told them all.

Helen was crying from her chair. Her children's thoughtfulness was touching. This Christmas it was all they had, but they gave it freely. It reminded her of Jesus' love, true agape love. Helen smiled with pride.

"Thank you, Father, for this Christmas. Thank you for my children, my husband and my life. Amen." she silently prayed.

Chad gave her a knowing grin. He was proud of his children, too.

"Well, you young 'uns better get on back to bed now that your bellies are full," Gabriel said. "Get lots of sleep 'cause tomorrow's going to be an exciting day."

Chad and Helen wondered what he meant by that, but said nothing. They helped tuck the children back under their quilt. With a hug and a kiss from their parents, the children settled in.

"I want to thank you, Mister Davidson, for that fine meal," Chad told him. "We've had a year of trials and our resources are low."

"The food was my pleasure to share," Gabriel answered. "And tomorrow, you can tell me about your trials. But right now, with your permission, this old man needs rest."

"Certainly, sir, my apologies."

"None necessary, son. I thank you for your hospitality. Ma'am," he said, nodding toward Helen.

She nodded in return, "Goodnight, Mister Davidson."

Gabriel laid out his coat before the fire. Removing his boots, he knelt down to pray. Helen and Chad readied themselves for bed as well so they would not stare at him and intrude on his time with

God. Helen went to the privy which was located behind a curtain in the far corner of the room. It made a small triangular space that gave a body privacy in their close winter quarters – embarrassing, but necessary. How she longed for the privacy of their outhouse with a guest in the home.

A short time later, all the adults were settled in. Stomachs full and bodies warm from the fire, sleep came quickly.

When Helen awoke the next morning, all was quiet. She looked over to the children who still slept soundly. A dull light shone in through the two small windows. Chad was asleep beside her. Then she remembered their guest. Helen raised her head a bit so she could look at him. There was no man, or bear coat on the floor. Helen sat up in bed. Had she dreamed it all? She rubbed her eyes and looked around. The plate for the biscuits was sitting empty on the table. Mister Davidson's satchel was gone. Helen frowned. Surely it had been real.

Rising from the bed, still fully clothed in her brown wool dress, Helen walked over to a window. Peering out, she spotted footprints in the deep snow leading out to the barn. Had he already gone? She turned back to Chad wondering whether or not to wake him. She noticed the fire was nothing but simmering embers. She would put more wood on, then wake him.

Passing the table, she looked down at the blue metal plate. Yes, there were biscuit crumbs on it. It had not been a dream. Helen pushed her long, loose brown hair behind her shoulders. She did not want it to catch fire. Carefully, she placed two logs into the stone structure. Soon, she would set a pot of water to boiling for the oats.

Just as she was backing away from the fire, the front door opened. Helen jumped with fright, making a noise as her hand flew to calm her beating heart. She recognized Gabriel's enormous warm coat entering. His arms were burdened with sacks, jugs and jars. She leapt quickly to offer help.

"Good morning," he greeted quietly as she took several items.

Helen gave him a warm smile. "Good morning." She set her items on the table, as did he. "What is all this?"

He grinned. "Breakfast, dinner, and supper."

Helen's mouth dropped open. She was speechless. Was he serious? Her hands began to tremble.

"I've brought buttermilk, tea, spiced apples, potatoes, ham, canned vegetables, sugar, flour, salt, beef, and jam for Naomi."

Helen's knees gave way and she slid to the floor. "Oh, thank you, Lord!" she cried out loud.

"Wha...?" Chad said, waking from sleep. He saw Helen on her knees and Gabriel stepping toward her. Chad was out of bed in an instant. "Helen?"

"Oh, my dear. This man is an angel of God! Surely he must be," she told him. "Look at all this food he has brought to us."

Gabriel kept quiet his intent to give them all he had – at least three months worth still out in his crates and barrels in the barn. It would keep them through most of the winter.

"Is this true?" Chad asked him.

"Yes, my Christmas gift to you. I know for certain the Lord sent this storm so I would lose my way. He must be taking care of my family, because He re-routed me to you. I feel it is His wish for you to have this food, all of it, including what is still outside," Gabriel answered sincerely.

Helen was crying. Chad was overwhelmed. He would have to swallow his pride on this one and accept Mister Davidson's charity. If he did not, his family would surely die this winter. Besides, who was he to deny God's plan? "Sir, we are in your debt. Thank you," the younger man said.

"Don't thank me. Thank God. He has provided."

"We do, sir. We certainly do," Helen concluded.

The three Jenkins children awoke to smells of frying ham and flapjacks. Helen quickly whipped up the batter. This morning they would have their largest meal in six months. Buttermilk and spiced apples completed the feast. Naomi was absolutely delighted. She insisted on sitting next to Mister Davidson while they ate. Michael then begged to sit on the man's other side. Johnathan was still content to sit on his mother's lap. Everyone laughed and talked as though they had known each other for years.

"I would like to ask if I could stay through Christmas Day," Gabriel asked Chad and Helen. "I'd love to not have to be alone for another holiday."

"You know you are welcome," Chad answered. Christmas was tomorrow, and this man had saved all their lives.

"We'd be honored if you would," Helen then added.

"Besides, it's not every Christmas we get a new grandpa," Naomi put in to the adult conversation.

"Or me three new grandchildren," Gabriel added. "Besides, I have a good feeling Santa Claus may stop by tonight. I sure wouldn't want to miss that."

Chad frowned. What was he saying? He and Helen had nothing to give them. He wished Gabriel would stop getting their hopes up. He looked up to see Gabriel giving him and Helen a wink and a nod. Chad still frowned.

After breakfast, Helen and Naomi made bread dough. It filled the one room cabin with the smell of yeast. The loaves sat rising on the hearth while the females prepared stew. A large pot was filled with the beef, potatoes, vegetables, water, salt and flour. The males entertained themselves with an old game of checkers. It had belonged to Helen's father years ago.

"Thanks for feeding my horses this morning," Chad commented to Gabriel.

"It was no trouble. I wanted to see to mine and my mules. All was well and I didn't want to wake you. I'm a very early riser," he explained.

"I am, too, in the summer time," Chad grinned sheepishly. "I take advantage of my warm bed during cold winter days and sleep as long as I can."

Helen felt a little blush fill her cheeks. She wished Chad had not said that.

"Say, Mister Davidson, can I have a ride in your sleigh?" Matthew asked.

Johnathan stopped playing with his stuffed dog made from scraps of old material. He wanted to know the answer to that question, too.

"Certainly, Matthew. We can all go if you like."

The children's faces lit up.

"The children don't have warm coats, Mister Davidson. I'd fear for their health if they went," Helen told him with motherly concern.

"Not to fear. I have five extra buffalo hides in the sleigh. You can each wrap one around you," he told her.

"Hooray!" Matthew shouted.

"Oh, boy!" Naomi gushed.

"Sleigh ride, sleigh ride," Johnathan chanted, making his play puppy dance around.

Chad and Gabriel went to the barn. They would have to empty the sleigh of all its supplies and hook up the team.

"I've never seen horses this big," Chad told him as harnesses were being adjusted.

"Clydesdales," Gabriel answered.

The team was ready. Gabriel led them into the snow-filled yard while Chad carried the heavy buffalo furs to the house. "Wrap up everyone," he told them.

Helen wore an old bonnet over her head. The material was faded to a dull gray-green. The children's heads and hands were wrapped with clothing to keep them warm. Each took a buffalo hide to drape around their shoulders. The oldest two stepped out into the snow. Old rabbit furs were tied to their feet for shoes. Chad carried Johnathan to the sleigh and put him in the back with Helen and the other two children. Chad sat himself in the front with Gabriel.

"Ready?" the man called to them.

"Ready!" the two eldest shouted. Helen nodded her head.

Gabriel popped a whip over the horses heads. The loud snap sent them shuffling through the snow. The sleigh skimmed over the ice. Every passenger had a smile on their face. Gabriel led them across the winter landscape to a tree far in the distance. He circled wide and turned the sleigh back towards the house.

"Don't go back home yet," Michael begged.

Gabriel answered, "We won't."

The horses took them past the house. Gabriel had all the children giggling when he asked them to wave at the donkeys in the barn. Helen admitted to herself that this was the most fun their family had had in over a year. Gabriel circled wide again. More giggling and waving to the donkeys as they made their way back to the tree. They circled the house in this manner three times before coming to a stop in the yard. All cheeks were pink from cold.

"Papa, can we go see the donkeys?" Naomi asked.

"I don't see why not."

Helen led the children into the barn while the men unhitched the team.

"Mama, are these like the donkey Mary rode on to Bethlehem?" Naomi asked.

Helen smiled. Tonight they would read the story again from their family Bible as they had every Christmas Eve in the past. "Yes, honey, they are. Just like Mary's donkey."

Naomi and Michael stroked the animals. "I think it's wonderful we will have donkeys in our barn tonight, of all nights!" the little girl gushed.

Helen agreed, "Yes, that is special. God has given us a Christmas we will never forget."

Michael grabbed a handful of hay and began to put it near the donkey's mouth.

"I wouldn't do that, Michael," Gabriel said quickly. "That one is ornery; he might take a finger off." Michael quickly dropped the hay and stepped back.

The empty sleigh was now in the center of the barn. All the children climbed into it, imagining all sorts of adventures.

"I'd better go check on the bread," Helen told them. "Chad, you'll bring the children in?"

He agreed. Helen entered the cabin, savoring her few minutes of privacy before they all returned. The men and children remained in the barn for an hour. Helen had time to put the bread in the oven, do a little cleaning, set the table, pray, mend two socks and read a little from the Bible. It was quiet time she treasured.

When they all returned, Johnathan was very fussy. Chad immediately put him to bed for a nap. "Children, time for your reading lessons," he told the other two. It was the only way they would remain quiet long enough for Johnathan to fall asleep. Gabriel sat with Naomi, reading along from her book of poetry. Chad read quietly with Matthew, letting him sound out words from the Bible. These were the only two books in the house.

Gabriel fell asleep in his chair. Naomi had to keep her giggles quiet. She continued to read silently as the smell of baking bread filled the room.

Late in the afternoon, a meal of bread and stew was enjoyed by all. Gabriel shared with the family stories of Denver. They explained to him all their trials and troubles the year had wrought.

Losing a baby, a twister and a fire, no wonder they were destitute, Gabriel thought to himself.

After the meal, Chad read from Luke. Naomi listened carefully to the Christmas story. She smiled when her father mentioned the donkey. All the adults shared fond Christmas memories afterward.

"I have to say, I thought this was going to be our worst Christmas ever," Helen confessed. "But God turned it around for good, and it shall be our best, thanks to Mister Davidson." Chad nodded agreement.

"May Matthew and I sing a song for you, Mister Davidson?" Naomi asked.

"Certainly."

Naomi and Matthew huddled together to decide on the song. They broke out in unharmonic chords of "Silent Night." The adults smiled, hearing the tune. Chad and Helen both knew their children had little musical talent. Gabriel was a good sport though. He pretended to enjoy it.

"Fit for angels! That was great!" he boasted when the song ended. "What other songs do you know?"

"Joy to the world, the Lord is come . . ." Naomi quickly bellowed. Matthew caught up quickly. Johnathan covered his ears.

When they finished, Gabriel told them, "That was just marvelous!"

Chad wondered if the old man was part deaf. "Say, why don't we all sing some now," he suggested.

Gabriel had a deep baritone voice. Helen sang soprano. Chad was somewhere in between. It was an enjoyable hour spent in song and worship. It was nearly eight o'clock when Helen finally put the children to bed. They could barely settle down from all the singing and fun. Thoughts of Santa Claus filled their minds as well. Helen watched as Gabriel took Chad aside. They spoke in deep hushed tones. After half a minute, Chad cleared his throat.

"Helen, dear, Mister Davidson and I are going out to the barn for a while."

"Fine. I have mending to do and some things to prepare for tomorrow's meal." Helen began work on her sons' pants. Both had holes in the knees. She had a little more scrap material from one of her old skirts to patch them with. Helen smiled as she sewed. God was sure looking after them. "How great He is!" she said under her breath. With Mister Davidson's gift of the food stuffs, they would survive until spring. Then they could start over somehow – plant a new crop, acquire new animals. Somehow, in time, maybe they could repay him for all he had done. "Lord we are so grateful for all you've done in the last day. Thank you. Please bless Mister Davidson for all the good he's doing for us. Bring his family back to him, God. Thank you for saving us through the winter. Help us to begin anew in the spring. Please keep bein' with us, Lord, like you said. Amen."

Helen continued her mending. She made a mental note to ask Chad to sharpen her scissors. The children were sound asleep, finally, by the time the patches were on. It had taken thirty minutes and Chad and Mister Davidson were still in the barn. Helen snacked on a piece of bread. Maybe, she thought, the men were sorting through the food stuffs. Gabriel was probably showing Chad what they could keep. What a great man Gabriel was, an angel really. Helen was pondering this thought when the door opened. When she looked up, Chad was smiling ear to ear. There was a gleam in his eyes like she'd never seen. He held a large bundle.

"You'll not believe what this is," he told her quietly.

She shrugged.

"It's a turkey!"

"A turkey?" her eyes were wide as walnuts.

Chad nodded. "Yes, for Christmas dinner. And there's four more in the barn."

"Oh, Chad!" Helen exclaimed as her hand came to her mouth.

"And he's giving us a dozen chickens, a side of beef, six hams, bacon, sausage..." his voice trailed off.

Helen sat down in a chair. She had not realized how much food was in that sleigh.

"And there's more. Potatoes, beans, rice, canned vegetables, a barrel of flour, one of oats, sugar, all sorts of everything. More food than I've ever seen. There's also buttermilk and apple cider."

Helen was speechless, stunned. They would never be able to repay him for all this. As if Chad could read her thoughts, he added, "And he refuses my 'I owe you'. I told him we could provide future crops for him to sell in his store, but he adamantly opposes the idea. He insists this is a gift from God, not from him."

"He's an angel of God, Chad. That's what I think," she answered.

"You could be right, dear. He does have the right name for it," he smiled.

Gabriel came back to the cabin a short time later with a second bag of food for Christmas day. Chad and Helen had placed the turkey near the fire to thaw. Helen gave their guest an appreciative hug. "Thank you, sir, for everything."

Gabriel patted her on the back. "Let it be a blessing from God."

A short time later, the adults settled into bed. It had been a fun, busy day, and tomorrow would be just the same. The children especially would be so excited about the turkey. Helen said her goodnight prayers, kissed Chad, and fell asleep.

Helen awoke early the next morning with an urgent need to use the privy. Quietly she tip-toed past the curtain in the corner. When she came out, the dim light from the simmering embers and the dull gray coming in from the window allowed her to see the shadowy objects on the dining table. She went closer for a better look.

Helen gasped. Covering their table were gifts of all sorts. Something for everyone, it seemed. And even the buffalo furs were draped over all the chairs and benches. Her heart beat rapidly. She looked at Gabriel, who slept soundly on his pallet near the fire. Helen reached out to touch some of the items. A warm ladies bonnet, trimmed in ribbon. A porcelain doll for Naomi. Books, at least seven of them. And shoes for the children!

"Oh joy!" Helen shouted, waking the household. "Children, come and see!" she called to them, rushing to their bedside. They sat up dreamily, wiping their eyes. As soon as they saw the table, they scrambled from bed.

"Mama, a doll. Just look at her!" Naomi cried out with delight. She grabbed the curly haired baby and gave her a squeeze.

Chad sat on the bed grinning now, having already known the secret Gabriel had set about doing during the night. Gabriel too, now sat grinning near the hearth.

"Look what Santa brought!" Matthew shouted, grabbing the toy train carved from wood and painted red, yellow and black.

The children looked over the table for more toys. Besides the books, there were slates and chalk, a bag of marbles, three pairs of red mittens, a bag of candy sticks, a harmonica, two brown caps for the boys and a quilted bonnet for Naomi. Helen knew what a sacrifice this had all been for Gabriel to give them instead of giving it to his daughter and her family.

Naomi pulled on the warm bonnet, turning her head to show it off. "Look at me, Papa."

Little Johnathan began to scribble on the writing slate.

"Let's put some more wood on the fire so we can see all these wonderful gifts," Chad said, walking toward the hearth.

Helen looked over the table again. Beside the navy blue ladies bonnet rested two new dresses, simple but warm. One was dark blue cotton duck, the second a black wool. She held one up. It was a bit large, but she could take it in. Next to the dresses were ten balls of yarn for knitting. "Oh, we will all have scarves and new socks," she told them. "Maybe even a new shawl for me and Naomi." The little girl smiled. Next to the yarn were two men's shirts, a pair of trousers, and some clothing for the oldest two children. Two new dresses for Naomi – a green plaid and a blue striped, both from heavy cotton. For Michael, there were two new cotton duck shirts, a white and a blue, and two new pairs of pants, one in denim, the other brown wool. Near the clothes was a stack of material, red flannel for new long johns, white flannel for new underskirts and drawers, a medium-weight, plum-colored cotton and a heavy gray cotton. She knew the gray cotton could be used to make Johnathan a new set of clothes. Helen fingered the spools of thread sitting next to the material. What fun it would be sewing this winter.

"Did you look in this box?" Chad asked.

Helen peered inside the open container. There were six bars of soap, matches, a kitchen towel, candles, lamp oil, writing paper and a pencil. It was so much. She smiled, but was speechless. She felt as though she were at the mercantile in town, looking over the wonderful merchandise. It was hard to believe this was all for them.

"Mister Davidson, you are an angel of God for sure. May He show you mercy and bless your life abundantly for what you have done. I thank you and praise Him. Merry Christmas."

"Merry Christmas," Gabriel returned simply with a nod.

Chad and the children joined in, "Merry Christmas!"

June 1876, six months later

"Hey, Papa, someone's comin'," Naomi called out. She could easily see the wagon traveling across the prairie from her position in the barn loft. She had been up there for half an hour playing with her pretty porcelain doll which she had lovingly named Elizabeth. They were having an imaginary tea party since Naomi had just turned nine and was wearing her new plum-colored summer dress.

"Can you see who it is?" Chad asked from below. He was trying to fix the handle on his hoe. He had some weeding to do in the vegetable garden. Thankfully, Mister Smart at the trading post in Hoyt had let him trade two buffalo hides, some canning jars, seven fruit pies and six newly captured rabbits for some spring planting seeds. They had a good crop underway and would soon be able to trade for a cow. The rest of the animals would have to come later.

"No, sir. I can't tell who it is."

Chad dropped his tools and wiped his hands. "Better go tell your mother we got company." He walked outside the barn and spotted the wagon coming from the northwest. He did not recognize the driver.

Helen and the boys came out of the house. Helen rubbed the aching muscles in the sides of her swollen abdomen. Four more months and there would be a new person in the family. She and Chad had already agreed on the name. Gabriel if it was a boy and Gabrielle if it was a girl. They had not heard from Mister Davidson since he left the day after Christmas. She hoped all was well and prayed for him every day. "Who is it, Chad?" she asked.

"Not sure, honey. Don't recognize him."

The man driving the wagon removed his hat and began to wave it back and forth. Chad saw that it was an older boy, maybe fifteen or so. The Jenkins family watched the wagon come closer and pull into the yard.

"Afternoon to you," Chad greeted.

The young man nodded. "Good afternoon, sir, ma'am," he greeted in return. "Might you be the Jenkins family?"

"Yes, we are," Chad answered for them. "How can we help you?"

He reached down to shake Chad's hand. "Luke Carter's the name, sir. I'm Gabriel Davidson's grandson."

"Oh, welcome, young man. It's good to meet you. Glad to hear you are well and safe after the winter," Chad told him.

"Yes, sir, thank you. I'm working for my grandfather now."

"That's wonderful. How is he?" Chad questioned.

"He's fine, sir. He sends you all his best regards."

"And your brother and sister and parents, how are they?" Helen wondered.

"My brother and sister and I are all living with grandfather now. My parents are still in Dodge City," he answered.

"I'm sure your grandfather is pleased to have you staying with him," Helen spoke.

"Yes, ma'am. Purely pleased. So are we. We get to go to church and school now. We couldn't do that before. And I get to work for grandfather in the summer time. And that's why I'm here," the lad explained.

"Well, come down and come inside," Chad urged him.

"First things first, sir. Grandfather asked me to deliver these goods to you. He knew he could trust me to find my way," he said with a little pride. Luke locked the brake on the wagon wheel and jumped down. He quickly untied a canvas covering and pulled it down. Underneath was a crate of four laying hens, a rooster, and a crate with two newly weaned piglets. Beside these was a sack of seed corn and hay seed. "That small box there is for you, ma'am," Luke said to Helen. "Grandfather says it's flower seeds to plant your own Eden right here on the plain."

Helen giggled with delight like a young girl. She took the box from Luke. "Tell him I said 'thank you'." Naomi walked over to get a look at the seed packets.

"Look at 'em!" Johnathan squealed at the sight of the piglets.

"Can we name them?" Matthew asked.

"Young Master Carter, I think there's no end to your grandfather's goodness," Chad told him, truly amazed. "He's given us so much already."

"Yes, sir. He told me what happened last winter. But he says, without you giving him shelter, he would have died in the cold."

"And we would all have perished without his food and warm clothing. We are even. I do appreciate all this, but . . ." Chad began.

Luke butted in, "Sir, if I may interrupt. Grandfather told me to tell you that all these things he gave you at Christmas was from God. Grandfather said he's been paid back sevenfold already for it. Now this here stuff is from Grandfather."

Helen started to speak but Chad stopped her with a gentle touch on the arm. "Luke, we humbly accept this gift. Thank you. And I'm sure we will want to write your grandfather a letter to thank him as well. You will stay for a day or two, won't you?" Chad asked.

Two days later, the young man left the Jenkins farm. A new friendship had been struck between them. It was agreed that their families would visit again in the future. Naomi ran up to the loft of the barn with a sheet of paper and a pencil. In secret she wrote out her thoughts.

Dear Diary. I met a wonderful boy two days ago, Luke Carter. He is so nice and Godly, handsome in the face, too. He is Mister Davidson's grandson and lives in Denver. That's not too far away. Papa promised we would go and visit there one day. I hope so. I want to see Luke again. I like him very much and I hope that he likes me, too. We are only six years apart - that is not too much. He would make a fine husband when I am older. I hope and pray that he will not find someone else before I am old enough. Wouldn't that be fine? Me, living in Denver, helping him manage his grandfather's store. What a good life that would be. God, I pray for it. Help me to grow up and be worthy of him, for your sake, Lord. We would make a fine pair. Thank you, Jesus, for hearing my prayer. Amen.

Naomi's Prayer

June 1882
Colorado

"Storm's brewin' this morning," Chad Jenkins told his wife as he entered their cabin with an armload of firewood. "The sky's all pink and there's a smell of rain in the air." He looked at the mantle clock. It was almost six-thirty.

"I'll wake the children to get their chores started," Helen answered.

Helen and Chad Jenkins had been married for sixteen years. Their cabin was forty miles east of Denver. It was a decent homestead, a good piece of land with crops and livestock. They had a barn, a smokehouse and a cabin with two spacious rooms. The first was the original cabin, now separated into three bedrooms by wooden plank walls and old sheets for doors. A wood-covered walkway connected the first cabin with the second room. A kindly neighbor had helped Chad build the new addition three years ago. It was now the combined kitchen and living area. It had a large fireplace, a cookstove, a table, two benches and four parlor chairs. Chad was particularly fond of the parlor chairs. He had traded several smoked hams for them. They were from a second-hand store in Denver, but were the nicest pieces of furniture they owned.

Only Naomi and Matthew, the oldest children were already up. Naomi was fifteen and a great help to her mother in the kitchen. Matthew was twelve and a great help to his father on the farm. Ten-year-old Johnathan helped as well, but he preferred mischief to chores. He was constantly writing and memorizing Bible verses to "strengthen his character," as his father put it. Sometimes he had to strengthen it on the seat of his britches. Next came the twins, Gabriel and Grace. They were almost six and learning to read and write. The last child in the Jenkins family was Simon. He was only two and loved pulling feathers off the chickens. He had to be watched carefully around all the animals.

Naomi had awoken on time and had dressed in her dove gray skirt and soft white blouse. Her brown hair was neatly braided down her back. She silently read her Bible verses for the day before her chores began. Proverbs thirty-one was one of her favorite chapters. She read it every week. "Dear Lord, please make me a woman like that. Help me to be worthy. Give me a husband who will trust me, that I may do him good all the days of my life. And if he happens to be Luke Carter, then I praise you for it, Lord. You know my deepest secret, my long time love for him. Please let it be so. Turn his heart toward me, so we may serve you together. Thank you, Jesus, for the hope that is in me. Amen."

Naomi heard the cabin door open. "Time to get up, children," her mother called. "Your pa says a storm's comin'. Get your chores done quickly." Helen then returned to the kitchen. Naomi knew her mother would need her help with breakfast, but first it was her job to get the twins and baby Simon dressed. She readied them and led them to the kitchen.

"Grace, you and Gabriel may set the table," Helen told them. Johnathan and Matthew had gone straight out to the barn to do their chores. Chad was out there as well. "Naomi, please see to the bacon," her mother asked. "Biscuits are already in the oven."

Thunder rumbled in the distance. Naomi knew her brothers would be in soon with eggs and fresh milk and water from the well. After breakfast, the children would all have to work on their lessons, then do more chores in the afternoon. Naomi hoped sometime today she could work on the baskets she made from prairie grass. It gave her something to trade for material and other things the family needed.

Heavy rains arrived just before noon. Naomi felt cramped in their cabin. She wished it were a sunny day so she could weave outside. Simon was crying about the toy train he wanted from

Gabriel. Grace was begging Gabriel to play dolls with her. Matthew and Johnathan were arguing about the marble game they played on the floor. Chad was trying to play a tune on the harmonica. Naomi wanted to scream.

She stood abruptly. "I just remembered a skirt I need to mend." Quickly she left the noisy room. Outside under the wooden porch, she breathed in the cool, damp air. Just a few minutes of peace was all she needed. Her thoughts drifted to Luke's last visit. It had been a whole year ago. The grandfather, that he and his brother and sister lived with in Denver, had remarried. Gabriel Davidson had closed his mercantile for two weeks to take his new wife, Margaret Strickland, on a train ride through Colorado. He told the grandchildren they could go out to the Jenkins' place if they wanted to. Luke brought them out for ten whole days.

Naomi sighed. Luke would be twenty-one now. There was a six-year difference between them, but that did not bother her any. She wondered if he had changed much in a year. "If only I could see you again . . ." she wished. Naomi leaned against the cabin wall staring out into the rain and across the land. Her thoughts took her to another place.

One week later a letter arrived. Mister Isaac Martin, the neighbor who had helped Chad build the new cabin, had gone into Denver to buy another plow horse and look for a woman to wife. He brought the letter back from Gabriel and Margaret Davidson.

Chad invited the colored man in for a visit. "Helen's got a good stew on for supper. Why don't you stay and visit a while."

"Don't mind if I do," the thirty-five-year-old said. "There's nothin' I hate more than havin' to eat my own cookin'." he grinned wide.

"Tell me all about Denver," Chad encouraged. "Find that wife you wanted?"

"Naw. Not much to choose from, but I sent off for one," he answered.

Chad and his wife gave Isaac a strange look. "What do you mean?" Chad asked for them all.

"Mail order bride. They got some colored ones in St. Louis. I paid my money and sent off for one. She'll be here August first," he said proudly.

"Isn't that a little risky, Mister Martin?" Helen worried.

"Naw, ma'am. Just takes faith. The good Lord above's been watchin' out for me real good since the big war. I got my freedom. I got my land. Now, I need a wife. It ain't good for man to be alone. It says that in Genesis. So I know Jesus had a wife picked out for me. He'll send her, August first."

Helen smiled. That was faith indeed, to marry a stranger. "I hope the Lord blesses you, Mister Martin," Helen told him.

"Me, too, ma'am," he answered grinning. "Me, too. Oh, speaking of mail, I got a letter for you all from Mister Davidson."

The children all crowded around as Isaac searched through his parcel. "Here it is."

Helen opened the paper. "Dated June seventh," she said. "'Warmest greetings, Jenkins family. Gabriel and I and the children are well, hope this letter finds you the same. Please thank Mister Martin for delivering this for me, as this is a letter of significance for your sweet Naomi. Mister Davidson and I would like to invite her to live with us for the duration of a school year beginning this August. Betsy would be most pleased to share her school and friends. Also, I will be starting Betsy's lessons in social graces this fall. Naomi might enjoy those as well. Please pray about it as it would be our pleasure to have her with us. She might enjoy attending church services every Sunday as well as the fellowship of others her age. Warmest regards, Margaret."

Helen looked at Chad, then at Naomi. Their daughter was grinning from ear to ear. "Oh, Mother, may I? Please? I would love to go." Not only would she get to go to school for the first time, but she would get to see Luke every day. Luke's sister, Betsy, was only one year older than she was. They would have the best time.

"It does sound like a good opportunity for you, but your father and I will discuss it later," Helen answered. She then turned to their guest, "Mister Martin, thank you for bringing the letter. Come on inside and have supper with us."

Naomi prayed hard. Her parents had said nothing about the letter. She wanted to go to Denver so badly. She could just imagine herself being there. Oh, what a joy!

Finally after two weeks, Chad and Helen sat her down. "Naomi, we have decided to let you go to Denver to school," her father told her.

"Thank you, Lord," the girl spoke out loud.

Her parents smiled. "We had much to consider. Your mother has a lot to take care of with six children. With you gone, her work will be doubled because you do so much. However, we realize this schooling will give you a better future and will open doors of opportunity for you. Who are we to keep you from knowledge? So, you may go with our blessing."

Naomi jumped up from her seat. She hugged both her parents around the neck. "Thank you, Ma and Pa. I won't let you down."

July twenty-ninth, Isaac Martin stopped by the Jenkins' house on his way to Denver. He was off to fetch his bride. Naomi handed him a letter to the Davidsons. "Please give this to them for me," she asked.

"Is you going to go there for school?" he asked, taking the paper.

"Yes, I am, Mister Martin. Papa is taking me in two more weeks. That's what's in the letter. I have to let them know I'm coming."

He smiled. "Good for you, young miss. You must be about as excited as I am today."

"Yes, sir. I can't wait."

Isaac tipped his hat. Her father was coming out of the house. "Mister Jenkins," he greeted.

"Isaac. Have a good trip. I'll see to those animals of yours," Chad told him. "And there'll be a good-sized smoked ham waiting for your return. It's our wedding gift."

"I thank you kindly, sir," the neighbor answered. He looked around. "Is Misses Jenkins home? I'd like to ask her opinion on somethin'."

Chad grimaced. "She is, but ain't feeling her best today."

"Oh," Isaac answered with obvious disappointment.

"Can I help?" Naomi questioned.

Isaac turned back to her. "You might. I was wondering, what would be a good gift to give my new bride. I don't know much about women folk. Been around men mostly all my life."

Naomi nodded. "Well, let's see. Yard goods are always useful. She can make clothes from them, or curtains, or linens for the table. But it's always nice for a lady to have a sweet scented bar of soap for bathing and such."

Her father cleared his throat. Naomi turned a slight shade of pink.

"That will do, child," he scolded.

"Well, I thank you for the advice, Miss Naomi," Isaac answered. He then turned to Chad. "We'll be by before you head to Denver so you can meet my bride." He tipped his hat again. "Give my regards to Misses Jenkins, I hope she's feeling good again soon. So long."

"Good luck. We'll be praying for you," Chad called.

All the Jenkins children waved and followed behind the wagon as Mister Martin left. Naomi thought happily that in just two weeks, it would be she who was leaving for Denver.

Isaac Martin arrived in Denver July thirty-first. He delivered the letter to the Davidsons and let them know he was in town for a day or two. Gabriel offered to let him sleep in their home, but Isaac refused.

"I have my wagon not too far away. I plan to sleep there tonight. Thank you, sir," Isaac declined. "But I would like to ask that my bride be able to stay here tomorrow night. I want to give us a day before the wedding, just to make sure we like each other."

Margaret smiled. "It must take a great leap of faith to do this," she told him.

"Yes, ma'am, that's what Misses Jenkins said. But I told her that the good Lord is watchin' over me. He's gonna send me a great young woman."

"Yes, I suspect he will," Gabriel agreed. "Have you seen the minister yet?"

"No, sir."

"Come, I will take you to him. Luke, watch the store for me."

Early the next afternoon, Luke went with Mister Martin to the train station. Isaac had purchased several gifts from the mercantile, including yard goods and soap scented with honeysuckle. Isaac paced back and forth on the platform. He did not even know her name, but she would be arriving within half an hour. Butterflies did somersaults in his stomach, but he tried to act calm. His purchases included a thin silver ring for his bride to wear after they were married. He hoped she would be pleased.

The train whistled from the distance. A cold sweat ran down Isaac's neck. This was it. He removed his hat to show manners. The train came to a slow stop. The passengers began to get off. Isaac strained, searching the platform. There was no colored woman.

"Lord, where is she?" he asked. "Please let her be safe." Isaac went to one of the railroad employees to ask of her whereabouts.

"No, haven't seen one," he was told.

Isaac's heart fell. Where could she be? "When's the next train?" he asked.

"Not 'till tomorrow."

Dejected, Isaac returned to Luke. "She's not here. They haven't seen her. The next train comes tomorrow. Guess I'll wait."

"Would you like to come to the store?" Luke asked.

He replaced his hat. "Maybe in a little while. Think I might wander 'round town for a spell." Isaac refrained from telling them he wanted some time alone to talk with God.

Luke watched as the man slumped his shoulders. It was obvious he was disappointed. Maybe she had just missed her train. Surely she would arrive tomorrow.

When the new bride failed to arrive on the second day, Isaac was beside himself. He sent a telegraph to the company handling the whole affair. He waited outside the office three hours for a reply. Finally, it came. "Mister Martin. Bride's whereabouts unknown."

God had promised him a bride, Isaac was sure of it. He just didn't understand what was happening. He could only stay in town another day or two, then he would need to get back to the homestead. He returned to the Davidson's store to tell them the news.

"How long will you stay in town?" Gabriel asked.

"Day after tomorrow. I'll check the station both days, then leave if she still doesn't show." There was a moment of silence. "I just wish I knew what happened to her."

That night, Isaac lay in his tent calling out to the Lord, "Sweet Jesus, it's not good for man to be alone. It says so in your word. I need my helpmate. Please help me to understand why this is happening. Amen."

The third day passed and still no bride. The Davidsons were greatly disappointed for Mister Martin. They prayed for him all evening. Gabriel could not understand why a man with such a heart for God would be going through such a trial. Then he remembered his dear friends the Jenkins. They had suffered three trials in one year, but it had brought about much joy and happiness in the end. Through suffering, God had allowed their two families to meet, and much good had come of their friendship. "Thank you, Jesus, for giving me this thought. I will share it with Isaac tomorrow."

Gabriel shared his hope with Isaac the next day. He reminded him that Christ works all things for good, even through times of trouble. Isaac knew that to be true, but it was still hard to bear. "We will see. My wagon is packed. I will go by the station this afternoon. If she is not there, I will return home."

Isaac delayed. He dreaded seeing that platform empty, again. Half an hour after the train arrived, he mustered up the courage to look. With slow steps, he walked up the street. When he stepped onto the platform, he saw a lone figure sitting on a small trunk. A colored woman. Her head was bowed into lace-gloved hands. She was crying. Isaac could see her body sobbing. He quickened his steps.

"Hello," he said.

The woman sniffed, trying to stop the tears. She looked up timidly.

Isaac removed his hat. She had a round face. He smiled. "Are you the mail order bride?" he asked.

She nodded.

Isaac's smile widened. "Thank you, Jesus!" he said under his breath. "I am Isaac Martin. Pleased to met you."

The young woman composed herself and stood. She offered her hand. "Opal May King."

"Why were you crying?" Isaac asked her.

"Because nobody was here to get me. I didn't know what I was gonna do. I thought for sure you had come and gone four days ago. I know I'm late, but it couldn't be helped," she told him.

Isaac waited for her to continue with an explanation.

"My sister was . . ." she paused and looked at the wooden floor beams. "Because she was havin' a child. The end came and it was bad. That was the day I was supposed to leave. I tried to help her, but she died." Opal's face looked very sad. "I had to get her buried next to our papa and mama. There's a little Negro cemetery in Missouri."

Isaac closed his eyes. He was ashamed. He should have had more faith. Her reason for being late was a very good one. "I am sorry about your sister. What of the baby?"

Opal shook her head.

"That's too bad. But I'm real glad you finally got here. I was real worried about you."

She gave him a weak smile. It was obvious she was fatigued from the stressful week.

"Are you hungry? My friends, the Davidsons, are putting you up for the night. They're white, but real nice folks. Here, let me take your trunk."

Isaac took the small box. It was no more than eighteen inches long and only a foot tall. She didn't have much. He led the way down the street to the store.

"Where in Missouri are you from?" he asked.

"St. Louis. I worked there," she answered. She was ashamed to tell him she scrubbed floors and washed glasses in a saloon. She overheard two men one day talking about mail order brides. She went that very day to the company they were talking about and signed up. Opal knew she needed a better life, one that didn't cause her shame. She ran away to her sister's shack while she waited. Her sister was a wash woman who lived by the river. She had been misused by some bad men at the docks. The baby was a result of that. Opal had a hard time understanding why her sister's life had been so full of misery, only to be cut short at the early age of twenty-three. Opal knew this was the right decision. She needed a new life. A clean start.

"Here we are," he told her.

Isaac took Opal into the mercantile and introduced her to everyone. They were extremely cordial, taking her into the back of the house. Margaret set a table for two in the kitchen, giving them both a hearty meal of chicken and dumplings with vegetables on the side. She even offered two glasses of cold lemonade to wash it down. "There's huckleberry pie on the counter when you're done."

Opal smiled. It was the best meal she'd had in a long time. And never before had a white lady treated her so well. "Thank you, ma'am," she told her.

Margaret smiled. "It's the least we can do. I've you a nice room off the back here. There's fresh water for washing and you may join us in the parlor tonight after we close the store."

Opal was intimidated. This was unfamiliar territory.

"Is this where I'll be livin'?" she asked.

Isaac shook his head. "No. Your new home is with me on my homestead, 'bout forty miles southeast of here. I've land and animals and crops. You'll like it. It sits on a bit of a hill and you can see for miles."

"Guess I'll leave you two to get acquainted," Margaret told them. "I'll be in the store if you need me."

Isaac and Opal made small talk for half an hour while they ate. When the meal was through, Isaac asked, "Do you think you will like it here? With me, I mean? I can pay for you to go home if you want, although, I can say, I would like you to stay."

She was obviously shy. "I will stay with you."

Isaac was elated. "I will treat you real good, I promise. I prayed for you. I knew God would send me the right one. I'm glad you came."

Opal smiled while a few tears filled her eyes. "I don't pray too much, but I'm sure glad you sent for me."

"You don't pray? Don't you believe in Jesus?" he asked. This was important.

She shrugged. "No one never told me 'bout Him. I heard of Him and all, but don't really know anythin' about it."

Isaac right away began to tell her about Jesus and how He saves people. He told her about all the miracles that He did, about the Bible and how God made everything. He told her how Jesus was born of a virgin in a manger. He told her about the Trinity and about being baptized. "I read the Bible every day so I can learn more. There is so much to know. It will change your life. He will make it good, all things for good," Isaac assured her. "It's real important that you believe too before we get married. I used to work as a cowboy and one of the men in the outfit told me about Jesus. Right then I started believing in Him and He's done some things for me. You can't see Him, but He's real. Will you believe, too?"

"Will you teach me? How to believe?" she asked.

"Yes. And how to pray," he told her.

"And how to read? No one ever taught me," she told him.

"Yes, and how to read. We will read the Bible together every day."

Opal smiled and nodded. Yes, this was going to be a good thing. She was glad now for sure that she had left her old life behind.

That night after Isaac left for his wagon, Margaret took Opal to the back room. A soft bed with a warm coverlet greeted her.

There was a lamp by the bedside and a large wash basin on the floor. Margaret had laid out new clothing on the bed. They were practical clothes, a brown striped skirt made from sturdy cotton and an off-white cotton blouse, a new pair of black stockings and some beige undergarments. A sturdy pair of new black work shoes rested on the floor as well.

"It's our gift for your wedding," Margaret told her. "Mister Davidson and I would like you to have it. We gave Isaac a new shirt and hat as well."

Opal gingerly touched the lovely clean fabric. She had not had new clothes in so long. "Thank you, ma'am," she answered quietly.

"Why don't we get you a bath, then you can rest. I'm sure you are tired. In the morning, Betsy will help you get ready. The minister will be here at nine."

"Yes, ma'am."

"There's just one more thing," Margaret added. She was curious to know. "How old are you, Opal?"

"Almost nineteen, ma'am."

The next morning, Betsy put blue ribbons into Opal's hair. The young woman's face lit up with excitement. "Is Mister Martin really a good man?" she asked her sixteen-year-old helper.

Betsy pulled a hairpin from her mouth. "Yes, he is. He lives near my good friend, Naomi Jenkins. He helped her family build a new cabin. I've never seen his place, but Naomi said it's a big cabin with a wide porch on all four sides."

"Where did he come from?"

Betsy shrugged. "Somewhere down south is all I know. He was a slave before the war, when he was a boy. The war ended when he was eighteen. He worked his way west and ended up here. That's all I know."

Opal did a little math on her fingers. "That means he's thirty-five now."

Betsy nodded as if this was nothing unusual. Opal gulped. She was half his age.

The ceremony was brief but pleasant. It took place in the Davidson's parlor, with a meal in the dining room afterward. Isaac wore his new shirt and was pleased with Opal's new clothes as well. She was thrilled when he pulled the ring from his pocket to place on her finger. Real tears spilled from her eyes.

"I feel so rich now," she whispered to him afterward.

Isaac was pleased with her reaction, as he had hoped. He was proud and pleased that God had blessed him so well with such a wife. He would do his best for her.

Naomi rolled her eyes at her sister. "Grace, get off the bed," she ordered for the third time. Naomi was trying to pack and Grace kept rolling over the bed, across all the clothes and onto the satchel. "I have to get this done before supper."

Grace rolled again, giggling. "That's it!" Naomi shouted. She picked up her sister and moved her bodily from the bed. Naomi walked outside, carrying the squirming girl who protested at the top of her lungs. "Now stay outside or I'm going to put you in the pigpen."

The five-year-old made a face and stuck out her tongue.

Naomi spun on her heels and went back to finish. She had the winter coat to pack, two wool dresses, an apron, a shawl and her only other summer dress. The dress and underthings she wore now, she would wear tomorrow. That, plus her calico prairie bonnet. Naomi let out a sigh. Everyone in the city would know she was a prairie girl. Her clothes gave it away. Naomi thought of Betsy's pretty dresses. "Lord, I know that I should be content to be clothed with your righteousness and humility, but the Proverbs thirty-one woman had red and purple silk. Please, can't I have a pretty dress, too?"

Three days later, Chad led their family wagon along the streets of Denver. Naomi sat by his side, eager to see the Davidsons. Matthew and Johnathan had wanted to come along too, but they were needed to stay and take care of the farm. Their mother needed them too, for Helen was in the family way again and not feeling well. They had not told any of the children yet.

Naomi bounded up the three front steps into the store. She spotted Margaret Davidson counting yard goods on the shelf. "Misses Davidson!" she called out with excitement.

Margaret smiled and put down her pencil and paper. She ran to embrace their new house guest. "You are here!"

"Yes, ma'am."

"And your family, are they all here?"

"No, ma'am. Just Papa and myself. Mama ain't feeling too good and the boys had to take care of the animals and the garden. They're none too pleased for it," the girl answered.

Margaret grinned. "No, I'm sure they're not. Betsy is in the house. I'm minding the store while the boys and Mister Davidson are out running an errand. They will be back soon. Run along and find Betsy."

Naomi took off through the door that connected the store to their home. "Betsy!" she called out.

"Naomi!" she heard her friend cry from the next room.

It was a sweet reunion. Both friends hugged and cried. "I've missed you," Naomi told her. "I get so lonely out there on the plain. No friends for miles and miles."

"Well, you're here now. For a whole year!" Betsy told her.

Naomi helped Betsy finish stuffing the duck. They pulled out the four hot loaves of bread and placed the duck in the oven. "We can put the beans and potatoes on in a little while. Come up to my room, I have something to show you."

Chad greeted Margaret Davidson in the store. He the unloaded Naomi's satchel and his small bag from the wagon. "I've brought some goods for trading: a side of smoked beef, pork sausage, four cow hides, fresh butter and a dozen chicks," he said. "We've more than we know what to do with. Helen sends you her best. I know she would have enjoyed a trip into town."

Margaret nodded. "I would have liked that, too. I'll be sure to send her a letter on your return. Thank you for the goods. You may put them in the storeroom. Gabriel will see to them when he arrives. It should not be long."

Chad did as she instructed. It took him several trips to unload the wagon. When that was done, he had to take the horses to the livery for the night. When he finally made it into the house, Gabriel and the boys had returned.

"Sorry we missed your arrival, Chad. Luke made a big business deal with the railroad and we were delivering their supplies," Gabriel said.

The men shook hands. "Good to see you again, all of you. The family looks well."

"We are, we are," Gabriel answered.

Chad turned to Luke. "Good for you getting a contract with the railroad. You must be pleased."

Luke nooded. "Thank you, sir. I'm happy about it. It will mean a lot more business for Grandfather."

"Yes, indeed, he's becoming quite the business man," The elderly man boasted. "Going to set up his future nice and good."

Luke grinned. He was not one to boast openly about his accomplishments. "The Lord's just blessing us right now, Grandfather, that's all."

Chad grinned. The young man had a good head on his shoulders.

"Where's Naomi?" thirteen-year-old Steven asked.

Margaret answered, "Probably up in your sister's room."

"Excuse me, Mister Jenkins," the boy said, taking off to say hello to Naomi.

Chad and Gabriel wandered into the storeroom to go over the trade goods. Luke watched the store while Margaret went into the kitchen to start the beans and potatoes.

At supper time, Chad saw his daughter for the first time since she had leapt off the wagon seat. She was wearing a new dress of two shades of blue. There were pretty bows down the front and tiny white lace around the edges of the sleeves and neck. "My, my, what is this?" he asked her.

"Oh, Papa. Isn't it beautiful? God heard my prayer for a pretty dress. He gave me, well, actually Betsy did, four dresses. I'm ever so pleased," she said, twirling around. The length of the skirt came to several inches above the ankle. Appropriate for her age. She wore dark stockings and a pair of Betsy's shoes. A lace-edged petticoat peeped from the underneath when she spun.

"You look mighty nice. All cleaned up from the farm," he answered with a wink. She looked older, too. That was not necessarily a good thing. To him, she was still a little girl.

Margaret beamed. It had been Betsy's idea to give Naomi her outgrown dresses. They were still in very good condition. There were four for summer wear. Margaret knew the fall and winter dresses in Betsy's trunk would go to Naomi as well, at least six of them.

"And I have my own space in Betsy's closet upstairs for all my things. She has a looking-glass on her wall and a desk with lots of books on a shelf above it. Oh, Papa, I'm just going to love it here," she gushed, giving him a hug. "Thank you for letting me come."

He patted her back, pleased for her happiness. She was growing up, Chad had to admit.

"When does school start?" Naomi asked.

"Not 'till next month, thank goodness," Steven answered.

Gabriel frowned. "Steven."

The boy said nothing.

"The second week of September," Betsy answered. "I'm glad you came early. It will give you a chance to meet some of my friends. Cecile Warrick is having a party in a week. You can meet them all then. She told me her father rented a circus monkey for the party. It will be such fun."

The girls giggled and continued their conversation about future plans and events. The evening was spent happily in the parlor. Naomi secretly stole a glance at Luke from time to time. He was still as good looking as she had remembered, maybe even more so. He had talked with her father mostly at supper, but she had remained calm and conducted herself maturely. It was late into the night when Naomi and Betsy finally fell asleep.

At breakfast, Chad watched as his daughter entered the room wearing another new dress. This one was a soft mint green with beige lace trimming every edge and a pleated front. "Good morning, Father," she said to him with a smile.

"Good morning, Naomi," he answered. "You look nice today. I especially like what Betsy did to your hair. You've never worn it like that before." He knew his daughter would be hoping for compliments.

Naomi smiled wider. "Thank you, Papa. Do you really like the ringlets?" she asked, bouncing the long spiraled curls with her hand.

"I do."

"I think it's very becoming," Margaret added, placing salt on the table. "That dress fits you well. We might have to take it in just a bit in the sides. But we can see to that later. Come, girls, you are just in time to help me serve breakfast."

"Mmmm, smells good, Maggie," Luke said walking into the room.

Naomi looked up and smiled. He gave everyone in the room a grin. "You're looking mighty grown up, Naomi. Better watch out, your pa might take you back to the farm," he teased.

Chad chuckled. "You ain't kiddin'."

Gabriel entered and sat in his chair. When the meal was served, he blessed the food, and they began to eat.

"Grandfather, do you think you could spare Luke for a little while today?" Betsy asked. "I want to show Naomi around town and we need an escort."

Naomi's hopes grew.

"I'll go," Margaret said. "I've a new hat to pick up from Misses Clairborne's shop and I need to speak to the minister's wife about this year's autumn bazaar. I also have some bandages to donate to the hospital. You girls may help me." Naomi slumped slightly in her seat.

"Very well, then," Gabriel nodded.

"That is best anyway. I have another meeting with the railroad this afternoon. Maybe Saturday I can escort you young ladies to the park. Would that be acceptable?" he asked.

"You know it would, brother," Betsy answered.

Naomi looked at her father. "What will you do today, Papa?" She knew he was not planning to leave until tomorrow.

"Gabriel and I are repacking supplies in the wagon. Fall rations and things your mother needs," he answered. "That should take most of the morning."

"That reminds me," Margaret interrupted. "I've saved out some cloth for Helen that I'm sure she would like to have. It would make the loveliest blouse, or a little dress for Grace."

"I'm sure she would appreciate it," Chad answered.

"Betsy dear, remind me to get it after breakfast."

Naomi said goodbye to her father the next morning. She cried several tears as she waved goodbye. "Lord, keep us all safe through the year until I see my family again," she prayed.

A week later, Naomi dressed for the party. She had met several of Betsy's friends at church on Sunday, but they had not had much time to visit. Today though, at least eight young women would be there. Naomi wore a pretty lilac-colored dress with fancy pleats and ruffles. Small lilac flowers were embroidered on the material with small pearl-colored beads sewn in the centers. She wore two lilac ribbons in her hair as well and a new pair of ivory stockings. Naomi felt like a princess.

"Now first there's Cecile Warrick. She's the one having the party. Then there's Lydia Lyndsey, her father helps run the bank. And there's Martha Douglass, her father is in the railroad business. Next is Bessie Wilson, her family is from back East and they were in the mining business or something like that. They own some of the silver mines in Colorado. And there's Nattie Plummer, her family owns several businesses in town. Sarah Keller's family owns a big ranch outside of town, lots of cattle and horses. Gertrude Hutchinson's father is a lawyer here. Ella Gray is her cousin and she lives with her because Ella's father is a soldier. He's off somewhere, I don't know where. Last, but not least is Fannie May Hopkins. Her father is a doctor here," Betsy concluded.

Naomi shook her head. "I'll never be able to remember all those names."

"You'll learn them. I bet you know them all within a week."

The party was a grand success. Naomi had the time of her life. All the girls welcomed her, except for one. Bessie Wilson put on airs knowing that Naomi was really from the country. The food was remarkable, pastries like Naomi had never seen. And Cecile's father had hired a man with a monkey to entertain the girls. He had an organ grinder and played his music while the animal danced and tipped his hat. He even went from girl to girl holding out his hand for treats or money. They delighted in it. The girls told Naomi all about school, the autumn bazaar held by the church and the winter supper parties at the holidays. Naomi was enchanted by their lifestyle, so completely opposite of her mundane existence on the farm.

That night after the party, she asked Margaret for some papers she could bind in a book. Naomi wanted to start a diary to record everything that happened to her in Denver. She did not ever want to forget any of it. There were going to be such good times. She would have so much to share with her family next year. "Thank you, Lord, for these experiences. This is such a gift you have given me. Thank you again. Amen."

By the end of September, Naomi was settled into school and church. She enjoyed having friends nearby and living in the city. Her academics were coming along well, although history was her hardest subject. At home in the afternoons, Margaret was teaching both Naomi and Betsy how to act like a proper lady. She told them is would help them make a better marriage. Well-bred men wanted well-bred wives. She made them memorize Bible verses every week.

Let your speech be always with grace. . . . — Colossians 4:6

But the fruit of the Spirit is love, joy, peace, long-suffering, gentleness, goodness, faith, meekness, temperance, . . . — Galatians 5:22

A prudent wife is from the Lord. . . . — Proverbs 19:14

A virtuous wife is a crown to her husband; but she that maketh ashamed is as rottenness in his bones. — Proverbs 12:4

There were many verses regarding character and proper behavior. Naomi thought for certain that Margaret knew them all. She even required them to memorize and recite the entire first five verses of first Peter, chapter three. Naomi had not realized how much work becoming a lady involved. Not only did they have to learn the character of a proper lady, but also the movements. Margaret taught them how to enter a room gracefully, how to walk, how to go up and down stairs properly, how to serve tea, how to sit, how to eat, how to laugh, even how to sneeze. She even gave instruction in dancing. One evening every week, she coerced Luke and Steven into helping. Naomi loved these lessons. She and Betsy traded partners with each turn. When Luke took her hand in his, she just knew he could read all her thoughts. She would look up at him and smile and try not to step on his toes.

On the first Wednesday in October, Margaret pulled out all the warm winter dresses for cleaning and ironing. The weather was turning cooler and the elbow length dresses were not enough to keep them warm. She hired a wash woman to come every Wednesday to take care of their laundry needs. She was downstairs now ironing all of Margaret's winter clothing. Betsy would need some new dresses with longer lengths now that she was sixteen. Margaret pulled the clothes from the trunk and placed them on Betsy's bed. There were two that might still fit. Betsy had grown considerably in the chest over the last year. She would definitely have to have some new dresses made. They could take care of that this afternoon after school. The other five would probably fit Naomi. There was the burgundy dress with small pleats in the bodice and a large bow that tied at the back of the waist. Next came a warm two-piece dress the color of cooked pumpkin. Dark brown piping framed the seams of the bodice, sleeves and skirt. The deep orange and brown piping would be very becoming with

Naomi's dark brown hair. The third dress was a forest green wool. A dainty lace peeked from beneath the collar and cuffs. The fourth was a dark blue heavy cotton. The bodice was fairly plain, but the skirt was fancy with a pleated ruffle in the front and back. The last dress for Naomi was raisin-colored. The deep purple fabric had four wide tucks along the bottom of the hem and tucks in the sleeves.

Margaret then looked at the two dresses for Betsy. The wool dress colored deep yellow like butternut squash had a looser bodice. The tucks in the bottom of the skirt could be let out for length and a pretty trim could be sewn in over the lines where the stitching had been. The second was a rust-colored heavy cotton. It had been sewn for Betsy only last March, so it should still fit. The ivory lace at the neckline set off the pearl-colored buttons at the sleeves and down the back.

"So much to iron," Margaret whispered out loud. "Poor Ida. I sure keep her busy."

That afternoon when the girls came home from school, they were delighted to find Ida ironing winter clothes. "Oh, I'm so glad. It was cold in the classroom this morning. Mister Messina had a terrible time keeping the stove lit," Betsy told her step-grandmother.

"You sure do have lots of pretty winter dresses," Naomi complimented. Betsy thanked Naomi for the comment.

Margaret cleared her throat, "Actually, Naomi, Betsy will be giving you five of them. They will be too small for her to wear this season."

"Really, you mean that?" Naomi asked.

"Yes, of course. All except these two," she said, touching Betsy's dresses in the pile.

Naomi squealed with delight. "How wonderful. Thank you!" she exclaimed, embracing Betsy and then Margaret in a tight hug. "You are both so good to me. I just love living here."

Later that day, Betsy chose four new bolts of cloth from the mercantile: a brown plaid, a navy blue, a thin silver and purple stripe, and a gray-green, the color of sage. Margaret would take them to the dressmakers shop tomorrow and choose the patterns and trim. Betsy trusted her judgment, because Margaret had wonderful taste in clothing. Her dresses were all worn with a corset and bustle. They were so becoming and fashionable, even for a woman in her late fifties.

Announcements were made for the autumn bazaar at church the following Sunday. Naomi prayed that Luke would dance with her. "Lord, how do I get him to see me for more than just another sister?" she silently added. Maybe she could wear her hair up.

That week, Naomi decided to wear her dark orange dress with the brown piping to the bazaar. She would have Margaret pin her hair into a chignon at the back of her head. She would ask Betsy for a ribbon to wear in it as well. Betsy decided on the rust-colored dress. She was particularly fond of the pearl buttons and wanted to wear a gold hair comb that had pearls in it. Both girls knew they would look nice and were excited at the prospect of dancing with some young men. "Now remember girls..." Naomi teased in a high voice, "clothe yourselves in righteousness."

"We will!" Betsy answered, grinning.

The girls baked on Friday before the bazaar. Naomi made two loaves of zucchini bread, Betsy made two pumpkin pies, and Margaret made a double batch of squash muffins with a strudel topping. Half of the goods would be sold at the Ladies Society booth. There would be other booths as well, an auction, demonstrations and dancing. Such fun!

Saturday afternoon arrived. The town hall was cleared of chairs that now lined the walls. Booths were constructed inside the building and out. Makeshift pens were set up for the livestock to be auctioned. Gabriel had given Betsy, Naomi and Steven each seventy-five cents to spend. Luke had his own money.

"Look at all the people," Betsy commented as the family made their way to the hall.

"Just think of the money it will raise for the church," Luke told them. "Think of all the Bibles and hymnals it will buy."

The streets were clogged with wagons, horses and people on foot.

"Girls, we don't have to work our ladies' booth until two o'clock, but we must get these baked goods turned in before we look around," Margaret told them. She then turned to her husband. "We will catch up with you in a bit, dear."

Before they walked off though, Betsy looked up at Luke. "You will dance with us at least once, won't you, brother? You wouldn't want us to be wallflowers, right?" she asked thinking of Naomi and herself.

"Of course, I will," he agreed.

Satisfied, the young ladies followed Margaret inside the building while the men remained outside to look around and visit with friends.

Naomi enjoyed the first half of the afternoon immensely. She saw all the friends from school and church. There were so many strangers about though, people from far and wide.

Margaret and the girls had their turn working the booth. It was fun and they made seven dollars selling baked goods during their hour. Afterward, they decided to spend their own money.

"I want to buy that canary we saw earlier," Betsy announced. "It comes with a little wooden cage and everything."

The girls scampered away to make the purchase. Once she had it, she asked, "Naomi, what are you going to buy?"

She bit her lip. "I don't know. I have more than everything I need. I think I will buy something for my family for Christmas. Hopefully Papa will be by this month to sell his crops. He can take it back home for me."

Betsy was touched by her friend's generosity. "What will you get for them?"

"Help me decide. I'll have to get something the whole family can enjoy. And I want to get them something nice, that they wouldn't normally buy for themselves."

The girls spent nearly an hour looking over all the donated goods. At long last, they settled on a set of dishes. There were blue and white china, very pretty with only two small cracks in two of the teacups. One of the saucers was missing as well. "Never mind that, there's only eight of us, and this is a set of ten."

The man at the booth put all the dishes in an old crate. It was packed with straw to cushion the china.

"They will love it! Especially Mama." Naomi said.

"You know, Naomi, Grandfather gave me seventy-five cents, but I have another fifty I saved from doing some work in the store last summer. I would like to buy your family a pretty blue tablecloth. I saw one back there at another booth."

"Oh, Betsy, that would be just heavenly."

The girls carried both the crate of dishes and the birdcage. After buying the table linen, they found Betsy's brother, Steven, and coerced him into helping them take their items home.

Upon their return, they watched part of the livestock auction. Naomi was delighted by the man's fast talking. They were surprised when Luke bid on a horse. In the end, it was his.

"Why does he need a horse?" Betsy asked her brother.

"Who knows?" Steven answered. "Maybe he wants one of his own. Grandfather keeps the other two busy with deliveries."

Naomi secretly hoped Luke was not planning to go away somewhere. Hopefully he just wanted it to get around town.

After the auction, refreshments were served inside the hall. There was a long table with punch, meats, fruit, sandwiches and sweets. The minister of the church spoke before the assembly, thanking them for their fine help making this the best bazaar ever. So far, they had raised over seventy-five dollars. Whoops and hollers came from the people. Naomi grinned at the fun. She would have so much to write about tonight in her diary.

When the minister finished speaking, they all prayed giving thanks to the Lord. As he stepped down from the platform, men with instruments stepped up.

"Pair up, ladies and gentlemen, it's time for a reel," one man said.

The room cleared as men and women situated themselves for dancing. Betsy and Naomi looked at one another nervously. Boys circled the room looking for the right girl. Naomi caught sight of Margaret and Gabriel in the dancing area. At sixty-something, they seemed spry as ever. The music began as the partners spun around. Betsy and Naomi sat this one out.

The second dance however, was a square dance. Both girls were asked by boys from school. "Margaret didn't teach us this," Naomi told her friend, worried about the steps.

"Don't worry, just follow along and do your best," Betsy called out.

The room was filled with squares of people. At least ten. There was clapping and toe-tapping going on everywhere. Occasionally, there was a whoop or a holler. Everyone seemed to be having fun, including Naomi, until she caught sight of Luke. He was dancing with a young woman Naomi had never seen. She was well-dressed, obviously well-bred. Naomi wanted to be sick at her stomach seeing the way Luke looked at this pretty woman. "Oh, Lord, no!" she cried out in her mind.

Naomi finished the dance and returned to her place along the wall. Betsy stayed in, dancing three more times. Naomi declined her invitations, too upset to do anything but watch in disappointment as Luke danced every dance with this same young woman. Naomi watched the girl's silvery-blue silk skirt swirl with each turn. Her shoes were fine white kid leather. Her hair and posture were perfect. Naomi wanted to cry.

Finally, someone cut in. Naomi held on to hope. Since he was a gentleman, Luke graciously let the man take over. He then spotted Naomi sitting alone on the wall. He had promised her a dance.

"Finish this one with me?" he asked.

Naomi was torn, but she knew she had better accept. She nodded, not wanting to speak for fear he would hear the turbulent emotion in her voice.

He whisked her out onto the floor. When he took her hand, tears threatened to spill. He gave her a big smile. Naomi was silent.

"If I didn't know better, I'd say you weren't having a good time," Luke told her as they came together in step. "Why were you up against the wall? You look pretty enough today, so the boys can't be that daft."

His kind words were an ointment to her hurt. She smiled. "I was just out of breath, that's all," she fibbed.

"So you are having fun?"

"Yes. Right now I'm enjoying myself very much," she answered honestly. She hoped those words were not too forward.

Luke chuckled and continued the steps to the music.

When the song ended, Luke gave her a proper bow of thanks. "Come, there's someone I want you to meet. She's new in town. Her family only arrived yesterday."

To Naomi's horror, he led her right to the young woman in the silvery-blue gown. "Naomi, this is Patricia Thomson, from Chicago," he said. "Miss Thomson, this is Naomi Jenkins, my sister's little friend."

Naomi wanted to fall into a hole. "Sister's little friend," he had said. Tears threatened again. If it weren't for all of Margaret's training, Naomi would have run away crying. Instead, she curtseyed politely. "Miss Thomson," she said with a wavering voice.

"How do you do?" the woman answered in a voice as smooth as cream. She offered her hand.

Naomi shook it against her will.

"Naomi is visiting us this year so she can attend school," Luke told the lady.

"How very nice," Patricia answered. "Do you like it here in Denver?"

"Mostly," Naomi returned with a forced smile.

Luke then looked at Patricia. "Would you do me the honor of the next dance?"

"Why certainly," she answered.

"Luke, you're not being a gentleman," Naomi told him. "You are not allowing her to dance with anyone else. That is very selfish."

Both Luke and Patricia gave her an odd look. Naomi smiled smugly and walked away with her nose a bit high. She had told him!

Naomi sat the rest of the dances out. Betsy tried several times to get her off the seat. "No, I'm fine right here," Naomi told her.

That evening when the Davidson family left the town hall, Luke was missing. "Where's Luke?" Steven asked.

"He's escorting a young lady home," his grandfather answered.

"Guess he finally found someone that caught his eye," Margaret spoke out loud.

"She's really pretty, too," Betsy added. "I saw them dancing together."

Naomi held her tears at bay. She had had such high hopes for today. She had looked her best and had prayed for God's hand to be in her favor. Oh, why had things turned out so wrong?

Naomi neglected her diary writing that night. She crawled under the covers next to Betsy in the bed they shared. Silently, she prayed, and cried until at last she fell asleep.

The next two months were a strain for Naomi to bear. Luke called on Patricia several nights each week. He spoke of her highly to everyone. They were making plans to attend the Christmas celebration together at church. Everyone expected a proposal any day. Silently she bore the pain. Naomi wrote her private thoughts in her diary, only it and God above knew the truth in her heart. She kept it from everyone else in the family. More often than once she regretted not returning to the farm with her father. He had come in late October, as expected to barter and trade some of the year's crops. It had been a pleasant enough two day visit and Naomi enjoyed the letters from her mother. She had even knit her a pair of mittens for an early Christmas gift. They were warm, and Naomi appreciated them. But her father had returned, not knowing his daughter's private sorrow.

Naomi grew angry at God. He had given her a love for Luke that she would never be able to share with him. It pulled at her heart. There was little joy in the season. From the Davidson's she received a new warm burgundy-colored coat with a matching brown and burgundy bonnet. Both would last her well into adulthood. She thanked them kindly for their gift and gave them the embroidered handkerchiefs she had worked on throughout the season. All carried the initials of the recipient. Everyone showed appreciation except for Steven. The lad didn't care much for embroidered handkerchiefs.

Luke went visiting Patricia Thomson on Christmas Day. After church services that afternoon, he left. The Davidsons ate their meal without him. Naomi honestly tried to have a good time, enjoying the company and the fine meal. But her heart was not in it. Her prayers had grown empty. She was not right with God.

When Luke returned that evening all smiles, Naomi feared the worst. Surely he had come to an understanding with Patricia today. Their engagement would probably be announced by year's end. He showed everyone the fine cuff links she had given him. And she had liked the bottle of perfume he had given her. Naomi excused herself, not wanting to hear more, and went to bed.

When no announcement came of an engagement, Naomi was a little cheered. She, Betsy and Steven returned to school, even during the dead of winter. The snow was deep and the air bitter cold. Naomi was greatly thankful now for her new warm coat and bonnet. She hoped her family back home was warm. She thought of them more and more. As much as she truly enjoyed her friends in the city, she missed her family.

Come February, Luke was seldom home. During the day, he worked in the store, then at night he left for the Thomson's home. Naomi seldom saw him. It did little to lessen the ache in her heart. She was kept busy with school work and Margaret's lessons at home. And she had her chores in the house, but still, her mind wandered.

Then one day after school, she and Betsy entered the store. Naomi saw Luke looking over the wedding rings they had in stock. She took off running for her room. Tears ran down her face as she shut the door. Utter defeat filled her mind. It was hopeless. Betsy came in to see what was the matter. Naomi refused to tell her.

Margaret came in. "We are worried about you, Naomi dear. Come down to the parlor and we will have tea. Pull yourself together and we can talk about it." Margaret expected her to obey, so Naomi stopped the flow of tears. Betsy found her a cool clean face cloth.

Down in the parlor fifteen minutes later, the three females sat in awkward silence. Margaret allowed Betsy to serve tea. She handed Naomi a cup. A small plate of scones rested nearby.

Margaret was the first to speak, "Naomi dear, now do tell what is the matter. Can we help? Do you miss home?"

Naomi shook her head. Tears threatened again. She stared into the dark tea. A sob escaped. Then another. Soon, she was crying over her fine bone china tea cup. Naomi placed it on the nearby tray and covered her face. Taking a deep breath, she told them what was wrong.

"I love him. I love him so much. I have since I was nine-years-old," she gushed through sobs.

"Love who, dear?" Margaret asked.

"Luke," came her reply.

Margaret and Betsy looked at each other. They had not known.

"And now he's in there looking at wedding rings. I'll just die if he marries Patricia. I've loved him for so long. I was so sure God had put our families together so we could get married. I've prayed and prayed for years that he would love me. I know God has a plan for us. I just know it, and he's going to go and ruin it by marrying that Patricia," she cried.

Having compassion for her friend, Betsy wrapped an arm around Naomi's shoulders. "I never knew you loved him. Naomi, why didn't you tell me before?"

"It was secret," the girl sobbed.

Margaret pursed her lips. "Naomi honey, I can surely appreciate why you love Luke. He is a good, young man."

"Yes, ma'am. I know," Naomi replied. "And I'm a good Christian girl. Why won't he notice me?"

Margaret felt pain for Naomi. She sat next to her and stroked her back. Margaret took a deep breath. "You are only fifteen, dear. He thinks of you as a lovely girl. Six years is a big difference between you and him at this age. I hate for your heart to get broken, Naomi, but Luke seems quite smitten with this Patricia, regardless of what we think of her," Margaret added.

Naomi sobbed again.

Betsy nodded. "You are a better choice, Naomi, I'll give you that. Patricia is, well, I'll just say she's not the Proverbs thirty-one type."

What went unmentioned in the room was that Patricia was wealthy and she used it to her advantage. Having the money was not the problem, but her demeanor about it was. She had an attitude that she was superior to everyone else in town. It was obvious that Luke was smitten with her beauty, her upbringing and possibly her money. It seemed hard to believe Luke could be swayed by such things, but he was obviously doing his thinking outside of prayer and fellowship with God.

Margaret cleared her throat, "Regardless, we should pray for her. For Patricia's attitude and for Luke to know God's will," Margaret made a mental note to speak with Gabriel about the situation this evening. Hopefully he could talk some sense into his grandson.

That night in bed, Naomi admitted to herself that it was hard to pray for Patricia, but she did it anyway. "Lord, I'm sorry for blaming you for everything that has happened. Please help me to know why Luke is loving Patricia instead of me. I pray that Luke will see what your plan is for him. I pray that he will pray about his future. I pray he will think clearly. Let him go to the Bible, Lord, for guidance and to his grandfather for advice. Give him the wisdom he needs to see that his choice in Patricia is not the right one. At least I don't think it is and I usually know your will, Lord. We're close you and me, well, except for lately. I'm so sorry. I'll get back in your word, I'll come to you for answers. You've always helped me before, even if it's not what I wanted, you've helped me to see it your way. And that leads me to Patricia. I haven't been charitable toward her like I should. Sorry, please forgive me. I pray that she might see how wrong and hurtful her attitude is toward others. Give her a gracious heart. Thank you, Jesus, for hearing my prayer. Amen."

The very next night, Luke came home early from his visit with Patricia. Grumbling, he plopped himself down on the parlor sofa.

"What's the matter, Luke?" Gabriel asked.

All eyes in the parlor were on him. He shook his head, not wanting to talk about it. Luke sulked in his big easy chair by the fire. He spoke little that night. When he excused himself to bed, Gabriel stood also.

"I want to speak with you about something, Luke," Gabriel told him.

"Can it wait, Grandfather? I've had a bad day."

"No, Son, it can not. Let's go upstairs. We can discuss it on the way."

Naomi's heart pounded. She prayed Margaret had not told Gabriel about her secret. She would faint from embarrassment if Gabriel just came out and told Luke that she loved him. Trying not to stare as they left the room, Naomi focused her eyes on some pleats of her dark blue dress.

"Lord, please let this all work out," she prayed.

The next morning at the breakfast table, Naomi learned from Betsy that Luke and Patricia had had an argument. Over what, none of them knew, but it had been a big one. Naomi looked at her plate. The two fried eggs and thick slice of bacon mirrored the smile on her face. "Thank you, God, I still have a chance!"

By mid-March, Luke had stopped visiting Patricia altogether. He concentrated his energies on work. He negotiated several big contracts for his grandfather, bringing the family more business. At night in the parlor, he read over scripture, searching for answers to his deepest problems. And he was not the least bit surprised one Sunday when Patricia's father announced her engagement to a man from back East. All eyes in the congregation turned to Luke, who had to grimace and bear their surprise. But he took it like a man, a man God would be proud of.

In April, Betsy celebrated her seventeenth birthday. She had a large party in the parlor with all their friends from school. Four young men were even invited. They gave Betsy and Naomi much attention. Luke watched from the corner with his grandparents as the young men in the room changed partners to dance with every girl. Gabriel encouraged him to dance as well, but he politely refused. At the end of the month, the family celebrated Luke's birthday as well. He was now twenty-two. His grandfather gave him the store.

"I'm getting too old to work all day. I need naps," the older man explained. "It's time for you to take over. I'll still be here, but you're in charge. You've proven you can do the work. And I've no doubt the store will continue to succeed."

Luke had a hard time accepting his grandfather's gift. It was a big responsibility.

"Before I take over, Grandfather, may I do one thing?" Luke asked.

"Of course, Son."

"I would like to take some time to myself. Go off alone. Spend some quiet time with God, just Him and me. May I have a few weeks?"

Naomi bit her lip. He was leaving. And she would be leaving too in June. Naomi took a breath, resigning herself to life without Luke. God had not done what she had hoped for all these years. She would have to accept it.

While Luke was away, spring arrived. May was clear and sunny and lovely. Flowers came up from window boxes, clay pots and gardens. Margaret talked Gabriel into putting in a brick patio behind their home, complete with benches, a small table and an array of blooming vines. It was where Naomi celebrated her sixteenth birthday.

Margaret bought her two new dresses with floor length hems. A modest bustle fit underneath with a pretty embroidered corset. The first was a pink and white stripe trimmed with rose-colored fringe. Naomi felt positively angelic in it. With her new straw bonnet from Betsy, she would be the perfect fashion plate. Even though it was not practical on the farm, she could hardly wait to show her mother in another month. The second dress was pretty sage green with small white flowers printed with on it. This dress was two pieces and trimmed with wide white lace. Margaret had told Naomi she could invite some friends over for high tea on the new patio. Margaret fixed her hair up all fancy and ladylike. Naomi wore her pink and white dress. When she entered the back yard, all her friends gushed at the new gown. Now she looked like a true lady. And she had the heart of a lady, too. One that was learning to be content with whatever path God placed her on. She had come to an understanding within herself that God had to come first, even before her own desires, including Luke.

The tea party was a delight. Margaret was very proud of both Betsy and Naomi for how they handled themselves. Their progress over the year was remarkable. They served tea and conducted themselves properly the entire time. All the females enjoyed strawberry tarts, English tea, raisin scones, meringue kisses, ham and watercress sandwiches, and salmon mousse. Afterward, Naomi gave Margaret an enormous embrace.

"Thank you so much, for all you've done for me this year. I will never forget it."

Along with the dresses and new hat she'd received, Naomi accepted several gifts from friends. One brought her some pretty sheets of writing paper, another gave a pretty hair comb with colored glass beads on it. A third gave her a pretty pair of soft kid gloves. They were white and very fashionable. Another gave her a new Bible with her name written in fancy writing inside. Naomi was truly content and thankful for all her blessings.

Luke returned at the end of the month. He had enjoyed his time exploring Colorado on his own. He had taken the train down to Colorado Springs and spent a few days there. He then journeyed around the great loop made by train all through the mountains. He told them all how beautiful it was and how he had come to an understanding of God's purpose for his life. He had so enjoyed waking up in a valley and watching the sun rise over God's glorious creation. He told them after this time of being alone in prayer, he was renewed and recommitted. He would henceforth do nothing without Christ.

Naomi was very pleased that he had found peace in Christ again. He was back to his old self, full of the fruits of the spirit mentioned in Galatians. Most especially was his joy. Naomi prayed the Lord would bless him indeed.

When Luke learned he had missed her birthday, he apologized. Later that evening, he entered the parlor with a small white kitten. There was a small blue ribbon bow tied around its neck.

"How sweet!" Naomi said. "Is it for me?"

"I helped him pick it out," Steven bragged.

"And you did a fine job too, Steven," Naomi told the thirteen-year-old.

Betsy jumped up from her seat with Naomi so they could see the kitten together.

"She's so pretty," Betsy said with a little jealousy. She would have liked to have one, too, but her canary might not like it.

"What will you call her?" Steven asked.

Naomi shrugged. "I don't know. Hope, maybe." There was meaning behind the name, of course, but she would not explain it. Naomi nuzzled the little creature.

Steven wrinkled up his nose. "Hope? That's no name for a cat. How about Snowball or Fur Ball, or Cotton Ball?"

Luke wrapped his arm around Steven's neck and pulled him away in the crook of his elbow. "How about we just call you Odd Ball?" Luke joked.

Under protest, Steven wriggled free. "That ain't funny, Luke."

"Sorry," Luke told him, holding out his hands in truce. He then looked at Naomi. "Do you like her?"

"Yes, very much. Thank you," she answered. From the corner of her eye, she noticed that Luke was grinning. And he was staring at her as well. A small smile crept into the corners of her mouth. Maybe the Lord was finally working in Luke's heart. Oh, how she prayed for it.

In June, Betsy graduated from school along with fifteen other students. "What will you do this fall?" Naomi wondered.

"I guess I will help Luke in the store," the girl answered.

"You may join me in the Ladies Aid Society," Margaret told her. "We can make bandages for the hospital, lend a hand at the children's home, make meals for the sick, collect donations for the needy, plan the fall bazaar. There's lots to do."

"I sure wish I could come back again this fall," Naomi told them wistfully. "It would be nice to finish school like you did."

"Well, why can't you?" Margaret asked.

Naomi looked at her quickly. "My mother needs me. I know it was a strain on them to let me go for this long. She has all my brothers and sister to care for."

Margaret patted her hand. "I will speak to Gabriel about it. Let us see what can be done."

Four days after school ended, Gabriel's wagon was packed with all of Naomi's things as well as gifts for the family. He would be returning her home for the summer, in the hopes that she could come back in the fall. Margaret suggested they provide a maid for the Jenkins family to take Naomi's place in September.

Naomi hugged everyone else goodbye on the front steps of the store.

"See ya later," Steven told her, not much affected by her departure.

Betsy, however, was in tears. "I will pray for you every evening at six," she sobbed.

Naomi cried, too. Margaret gave her a pretty handkerchief trimmed with embroidery. "Here, my dear. Use this. I hope to see you again this fall. Be a good girl this summer." Margaret's eyes filled with tears as well.

Luke stepped forward next. "It was fun havin' you here," he said. He gave her a warm hug and a kiss on the forehead. "Hope you can come back in September."

Naomi managed a smile for him. "Me, too. Thank you."

Gabriel helped her climb into the seat. In two days she would be home. She waved goodbye as the wagon pulled away.

Naomi was thrilled to see her family again after all this time. All her brothers and sisters ran around the wagon with excitement.

She was greatly surprised by the tiny new baby in her mother's arms.

"A new baby, Mama?" she asked.

Helen nodded and turned the bundle for Naomi to see.

"You have another brother," Chad told his daughter, helping her down. He gave her a warm embrace. "It is good to see you again, Naomi."

"Thank you, Papa. Hello, Mama," she greeted her mother with a hug. "What's his name?"

"Christopher Samuel," Helen answered. "He's two months old."

"And he cries a lot!" six-year-old Gabriel added.

"Did you bring me something from Denver?" Grace asked.

Naomi smiled at her only sister. "Yes, I have gifts for everyone."

Gabriel Davidson stayed for three days visiting with the Jenkins family. Out in the barn, he spoke with Chad about arrangements for Naomi to continue her schooling this fall. "I know it's asking a lot," the older man said, "but Margaret and I would like to have her with us a while longer. I'm sure Helen has a lot on her hands with the new baby, but if you will provide meals and housing for a maid, I think we can find a suitable helper for her."

Chad discussed it with Helen. They hated to see their oldest daughter leave again, but agreed to it for her benefit. Living in the middle of the plains was not much of a life for their daughter: no prospects for a husband, no friends, no schooling, and no church close by. Besides, it was obvious, she was now a lady, and being a farmer's wife was not where God was placing her. When Gabriel left the farm, he agreed to return the last week of August.

Naomi enjoyed her summer at home, but she dearly missed the city. Everyone in the family insisted each night that she read to them from her journal. It was full of all the wonderful stories of her exciting year in Denver. When Matthew and Johnathan were not helping their father on the farm, she even tutored them, teaching them some of the things she had learned at school. Johnathan did not much care for it, but Matthew was a good pupil. Helen and Chad were very proud of their daughter. God had blessed her with much. She was becoming a true Proverbs thirty-one woman.

Naomi helped her mother sew some new clothing for the family while she was there. Gabriel and Grace especially needed clothes. They were growing quickly and all the handed down clothing over the years was becoming too worn for use. As a special surprise, Naomi even altered one of her own handed down dresses from Betsy to give to her mother. It was the dark blue dress with pleats. She cut off the long sleeves, making them come just to the elbow. With the extra material, she made a panel in the seam on each side under the arm. It gave the dress ten more inches around the middle. Then all she had to do was take out some of the gathering in the waist and a few of the pleats in the dress to lengthen it. Perfect! Helen was delighted. It would be the most fashionable dress she owned.

As promised, Gabriel Davidson returned to the homestead in late August. By his side were Margaret and Betsy. Sitting in the back of the wagon was an older woman, dressed in plain clothes and an old faded bonnet.

The Jenkins family greeted them all warmly.

Betsy ran to Naomi, all smiles. "I've had the most fabulous summer. Wait 'till I tell you what's been happening," she spoke in high pitched tones.

The girls were distracted by Margaret and Gabriel. The older woman also had climbed down from the wagon.

Gabriel spoke first after the initial greetings. "This is the Widow Hammond," he said with a gesture to the older woman. "I've been telling her what a wonderful family you are and she is very excited to meet you."

Chad extended his hand. Helen greeted her as well with a handshake. "Welcome," she said.

The older woman nodded in greeting. "Hello."

Chad introduced everyone, beginning with himself and ending with the newest baby who was asleep inside.

"What a nice big family you have," she told them.

"Thank you, ma'am. The Lord has blessed us," Chad replied. He looked to his two oldest sons. "Boys, unload those bags if you would."

The dining table was moved outside into the yard. Betsy helped Naomi set it with the blue tablecloth and pretty blue and white dishes. They would eat in the fresh air this evening and enjoy the glorious summer sunset. The boys would be sleeping in the barn loft tonight to make room for their guests. They would only be staying for two days, so it was no inconvenience.

Mildred Hammond was fifty-seven-years-old, but still quite able-bodied. She had recently been widowed and left penniless. Having no other options, she had gone to the church for help. That is how the Davidson family had come to know her. They offered her the position helping out on the homestead this fall and she had eagerly accepted. It would be a roof over her head along with meals and safety. She had never had children of her own, so helping out with six would be a pure delight.

Naomi and Betsy offered to clean all the dishes so Helen could visit with Margaret. Naomi knew her mother secretly yearned for friends. They lived so far out, no friends were anywhere close. While wiping one of the cups, Naomi remembered something Betsy had said earlier. "What was it you wanted to tell me about your summer?" she asked.

Betsy grinned with the knowledge of her secret. "Well, do you remember Mister Broderick that moved into town just before you left? He came to church, the man was really tall with an enormous mustache."

"Oh yes, I remember," Naomi answered with a little laugh.

"Well, he has a family. A wife and four sons. They are all very nice. We got to know them well over the summer. His oldest son and I formed what you might call an attachment.," Betsy grinned.

Naomi's eyebrows shot up. "Really? You like him?"

Betsy nodded. "More than just like him, Naomi dear. I'm engaged."

Naomi dropped her dish into the pan of water. "What?"

Betsy giggled and nodded. "Engaged."

"No! You're teasing me," Naomi scolded.

"It's true, really."

"Betsy, you mean to tell me you met this man, and got engaged in just two months? How can you do that so fast?" Naomi demanded.

Betsy smiled. "When you know, you know."

"And your grandfather agrees to this? And Margaret? What does she think?" Naomi thought this was all just unbelievable.

"They like him too, very much. Jimmy went to them first and asked them. They said we had to wait until next year, but they agreed to it."

"I just can't believe it," Naomi told her.

"Aren't you happy for me?"

"Yes, just . . . very surprised," Naomi admitted. "What does he do? Hold old is he?"

Betsy beamed. "He's tall and broad-shouldered and handsome and he's twenty-one. His family is in business with the railroad. And he was educated back East."

Naomi smiled. "That all sounds very nice, but does he believe in Jesus?"

"Yes, of course. He even sings in the church sometime. He was in a quartet in college back east and wants to get another one going in Denver. Can you imagine? He even sings just for me sometimes," she added with a little giggle.

Naomi smiled. She thought about Luke. She had heard him sing in church. It wasn't so bad. She missed him very much. It would be good to see him again, although she would have to guard her heart more carefully this year. Surely he had found another young woman to care for since she had left.

"What news is there of Luke? I take it he is running the store single-handedly while you all are here," Naomi spoke.

"He's doing well. Grandfather says what a great job he's doing with the store. Luke has plans to expand next year and double the size of it. He's going to bring in a lot more products, manufactured goods and make it a real department store. Davidson's Department Store he wants to call it. He's already ordered the sign," Betsy told her.

"That sounds like he is staying busy. I'm glad he's doing so well," Naomi told her with genuine sincerity.

"How are you doing after that whole thing with Patricia last winter?" Betsy asked.

Naomi shrugged. "I've accepted the fact that I'm just his friend. If God wants us to get together, He will make it happen."

"He has not courted anyone else while you were gone," Betsy told her.

"Doesn't sound like he has time to," Naomi answered.

"That's true."

Naomi wanted to change the subject. She turned to Betsy and said, "So, tell me more about this Jimmy fellow..."

Four days later, Naomi was settled back into Betsy's room. She had again said goodbye to her family after helping the Widow Hammond settle into her room. Helen was happy about the arrangement, having an older woman as a friend was a blessing.

Luke was working in the store when they had arrived in Denver. A thunderstorm was brewing in the distance. The echo of the rumbles could be heard far to the west. Gabriel was quick to unload with Luke and Steven's help. Even the girls grabbed what they could before the rain came down.

"Welcome home," Luke greeted them all.

Naomi noticed he wore a fine new suit. He was such a dashing young man. That familiar squeeze on her heart returned. "Oh, Lord, no, please. Don't let me be in love with him. Let me get over it," She whispered under her breath.

"Any word from Mister Broderick?" Betsy asked.

"Yes, in fact, there's an invitation on the parlor table," Luke told her.

Betsy whisked herself away.

"Naomi, it's good to see you again," he added. Naomi gave him a warm smile.

"Thank you, Luke. It's good to be back. I hear you have great plans for the store."

"My sister has been filling you in then, I presume."

"Yes, she did."

"It will be exciting to see if I can pull it off."

"If it's the Lord's will, it will come to pass," Naomi assured him.

Luke smiled wide. "That it will."

One week later, Naomi met James Nathan Broderick the Third at his family's estate home in the very wealthy district of town. They were having a party for all their friends to officially announce the engagement of their firstborn son to Betsy Carter. The wedding was set for early April. Naomi liked James well enough. Betsy was obviously smitten. She could hardly wait to be his wife. She stood by his side for most of the party.

Naomi was introduced to his three brothers. Edward was twenty, Matthew was eighteen and Robert was seventeen. All were cookie cutter copies of their oldest brother. After refreshments and mingling, the fifty guests were entreated to play croquet on the back lawn or dance to the orchestra on the front lawn. All three brothers asked Naomi to dance. She obliged them.

"I like your dress," Edward complimented. "That shade of pink rose becomes the blush in your cheeks."

"Thank you," she answered, looking down at the pink and white striped gown.

When she partnered with Matthew, he complimented her dancing. "You dance so well. You have the grace of angel's wings on your feet."

Naomi tried not to snicker. It was a nice compliment, but he was taking the flattery a bit too far.

Seventeen-year-old Robert was full of praise as well. "I don't believe I've ever danced with anyone quite as lovely as you," he flattered.

Naomi was amused by the compliments, but did not truly believe they were sincere.

When she had gone through the brothers, Luke stepped up. "May I?" he asked.

Naomi allowed him the next dance. "So how do you find the Broderick brothers?" he asked her.

Snickering, Naomi answered, "Bubbling with praise and compliments."

"I thought as much. I overheard one of them telling two other young women the same compliment less than fifteen minutes apart."

Naomi grew concerned. "Do you think Betsy's fiancé is sincere?"

"I do. He's not quite like his brothers. Thank the Lord for Betsy's sake. The others just aren't mature yet, I guess," he tried to reason. "I just wanted to warn you about them. Don't get serious about any of them."

"As if I could be," Naomi answered before thinking. She bit her lip as blush rushed to her cheeks.

Luke raised an eyebrow. "Really? Well then, my jealousy at seeing them dance with you is unfounded."

Naomi's heart beat a little faster. She gave him a strange look. "Jealousy? Luke, be serious. Even I know you think of me as a little sister."

He spun her around as the music progressed. When they came back together he smiled. "I don't know, Naomi. You've changed since I saw you last."

Naomi stopped dancing. She looked into his face. "Luke, please don't tease me. My heart can not bear it. Not from you."

Luke's brows furrowed in thought. "I apologize. Shall we continue the dance?"

Naomi put her hand in his again and continued the steps. When the music ended, Luke asked, "Would you like to go play croquet or get some punch?"

"I think I would like to sit down now," she answered. "Where is Betsy?"

Luke took Naomi to his sister then excused himself. He had been dismissed. His mind played over their conversation. He had struck at something in her heart. He wondered what it was.

At home over the next few weeks, Luke found himself watching Naomi from the corner of his eye. She had grown up nicely into a pretty young woman. She was grateful and full of the love of God. She was a bit young still, but had certainly caught his eye. He would have to talk with his grandfather about it soon and get his opinion on the whole matter.

While Naomi and Steven were at school, Betsy and Margaret planned her wedding trousseau. There were many items to be made and bought. A wedding gown, and at least four other dresses, plus new sleeping gowns and robes. And there had to be new hats as well. Jimmy was planning on a two week trip to San Francisco after the wedding. Betsy was delighted. She would then be moving into his family's large estate. She was excited about that, too.

One night when the two girls were settling into bed, Betsy turned to Naomi. Do you think it is wrong for me to marry a man with so much money? In the Bible is says that money is the root of all evil," she said with a worried voice.

"Not if you love him, I don't think," Naomi answered. "And if he loves the Lord, too, and you use the money for good and not for evil, I don't see the harm in it. Think of all the people you will be able to help. Think of it as your gift from God. You have to use it for Him though."

Betsy smiled in the dark. Naomi always had a good answer taken from scripture. "I can hardly wait to get married."

October arrived with the fall bazaar. The Ladies Society this year decided to have a masquerade ball. During the day would be the usual booths, auctions, demonstrations and food items for sale, but that night, everyone was invited to the ball. A theater troupe was hired to perform juggling and other acrobatic feats. The men and women at the ball would have to wear some kind of mask. Everyone in town scrambled to find the best costume. Tickets were sold at a whopping two dollars per person. The church would be raising at least one thousand dollars to go toward a new building.

They wanted to start a new orphanage and school. It was a great undertaking.

A young man from school asked Naomi if he could be her escort. Disappointed that Luke had not asked her, she accepted. He was nice enough. There would be no harm in going with him, he was a friend after all. That night, Luke found her in the kitchen getting a little something to eat before bedtime.

"Naomi, can I talk with you?" he asked.

Not thinking much of it, she answered casually, "Sure."

"Well, I was wondering, if nobody else has asked you, may I be your escort to the masquerade ball?"

Naomi's heart sunk down to her shoes. If only he had asked her last night. She bit her lip. "Luke, I, uh. Well, you see, I would love for you to be my escort, but someone else at school today asked if he could take me. Since I'd had no other offers, I told him yes."

"Oh, I see," he answered, obviously disappointed. His timing had been very poor. "Well, maybe you will save me a dance or two?"

Naomi smiled."Yes. Certainly." Her heart fluttered. Was he finally coming around? "Please, Lord, let it be," she silently prayed.

The day of the bazaar, the entire household was bubbling with excitement.

"Aren't you going to tell us what your mask is?" Betsy asked of Naomi. She had kept it a secret these last two weeks. It was driving her friend crazy.

"No. I want it to be a surprise for you all."

"Mine is a tiger," Steven announced, proud of his work.

"I know, we've seen it," Betsy told him, rolling her eyes. He had bragged about his mask all week.

Luke closed the store at noon. He put a sign in the window that they would reopen on Monday. As he walked through the house, Naomi and Betsy were waiting in the parlor. Naomi wore her burgundy dress with pleats. Her hair was spun and pinned neatly in a chignon. A smart straw hat perched high on top of her head. She gave him a warm smile. Luke had to admit he was very fond of Naomi. He had prayed about his feelings a lot over the last few weeks. He had known her for so long, it was strange to have these new feelings. But God had given him a peace about pursuing her.

When they all were ready, the assembled family walked toward the main street. It was already jammed with people and animals. Denver had a population of over thirty-five thousand people. Luke felt for certain that at least half had come for the event. The women left the group to work their booth. Luke and his grandfather walked around watching the fun. Steven ran off with some friends. It gave Luke a chance to speak with Gabriel.

"Grandfather, there is something I need your advice on."

"What is it, Luke?"

"It's about Naomi. She's growing up and I've been thinking a lot about her lately. Do you think that is wrong?" Luke wanted to know. He trusted his grandfather.

Gabriel grinned. "No. She's a delight to think about, has been since I met her when she was eight. She's grown into a good Godly young woman. What have you been thinking exactly?"

"To be frank, about courting her."

"That doesn't surprise me, Luke. You see, I've been privy to a secret now for quite some time. And maybe it's time to let you in on it."

"You don't think I'm too old for her then?" Luke asked.

Gabriel shook his head. Luke looked at him, waiting for the secret to be told.

"Last winter, Margaret told me that Naomi had seen you looking over wedding rings in the store. She broke down crying, confessing her long time love for you. She was, and I think still is, certain that God put our two families together so you and she would someday be married."

Luke was silent. He had no idea. How could he have not seen it all these years? "And this notion has your approval?"

"Certainly, son. I couldn't pick a finer bride for you than Naomi. But I believe also, that God has picked her for you. So if your eye has turned to her, then I am happy about it," the elderly man answered.

Luke smiled and walked just a little bit taller. His future had a bit more purpose in it. That gave him a confidence he'd not felt in a long time. "Thank you, Lord Jesus, for showing me the way," he prayed in a quiet voice.

That night, Luke watched quietly as the young man from school came for Naomi. She had surprised all with her mask. It was a re-done bonnet, covered in dyed pink gossamer that came down even over her face. Pink feathers stuck up between the folds. She had somehow fashioned a neck and head with a black beak that turned downward. It was the best flamingo any of them had ever seen. She coupled the mask with her pink and white striped gown. Pink beads decorated her lovely neck to complete the costume. They all agreed, she had a chance at taking a ribbon in the costume contest.

Luke was the last to leave home. He wanted to surprise Naomi at the ball.

The contest was a delight for everyone. There were masks of animals of all kinds. Even one of Noah's ark with small carved animals wired onto the hat. One mask was a house, another a train, some were flowers, others were simply decorated with feathers or beads. One was a waterfall, another made to look like a gold nugget. Some were well done, others poorly made. The evening, however, raised enough money for the church to build the new home for children. It was a success.

Toward the end of the night, Naomi began to wonder if Luke still wanted to dance. She had not seen him all evening. In fact, no one had seen him. She had danced with her escort several times and even the Broderick brothers. Gabriel too had asked for a dance. She began to look around for Luke. Instead of him, however, her eyes rested on a tall man standing nearby. He was dressed in all black: boots, trousers, shirt, vest, cape and hat. Even his mask was black with two round holes where his eyes looked out. In fact, his eyes were staring right at her. Naomi backed up a step. He looked like a bandito. She turned to walk away, but he caught up with her too quickly.

"The next dance, Miss Jenkins?" he asked.

Naomi spun around. It was Luke! That was his voice. She gave him a delighted smile and began to laugh.

"Like my costume?"

"You frightened me," she answered.

"I just wanted to be mysterious," he answered. "I wanted people to wonder who I was."

"Well, it worked. I could not tell it was you."

"Care to dance?" he asked again.

Naomi nodded, giving him her hand.

"You look lovely tonight," he told her after several moments.

"Thank you, Luke."

They were silent for a moment. Naomi noticed all her friends were staring, wondering the identity of her masked partner. She grinned again. "Everyone is staring at us," she whispered.

Luke looked around, flashing them all a grin.

"If I kissed you that would really set them spinning," he teased.

Naomi giggled, but her heart hammered. Just the thought of it made her knees want to give way. She laughed nervously.

"Where is your escort?" he asked her.

Naomi looked around.

"I don't see him."

"Maybe he went home," Luke teased.

"He wouldn't leave me here."

"Would you mind if I took you home tonight?" Luke asked.

"I'd hate to be rude to Billy," Naomi told him.

"He will understand. I'll find him," Luke said.

Naomi wasn't sure what to say. She was still a bit intimidated by Luke in his costume.

After two more dances together, Luke went to find young Billy Houston. When he realized it was Luke behind the mask, he reluctantly gave up the right to take Naomi home. Luke was delighted.

At the end of the night, Naomi had not won a prize for her costume, but she had received honorable mention. Luke, however, won third prize. He was given the award, not for creativity, but because nobody knew who he was. He had mastered the masquerade part. Upon receiving his prize, he unmasked, to everyone's surprise.

Margaret and Gabriel left the party early with Steven. They were tired and he was too young to stay late. Jimmy would bring Betsy home, as Luke would Naomi. At ten-thirty, Naomi began to grow tired.

"Luke, I'm ready to go home now. It's been such a long day."

He offered her his arm. "We can go say goodbye to Betsy first, if you want."

After finding his sister, Luke led them out the door and down the street. There were still many people milling about. Home was only a few blocks away, but the night was dark and cool.

Naomi did not know quite what to say. This moment was hard to believe as she held on to Luke's arm.

Luke took a breath as if to speak, but said nothing. Naomi wondered why.

When they neared the house attached to the store. Luke pulled her aside. There was blue spruce in the side yard. He led her toward it.

"Where are we going?" Naomi asked.

"To the side of the store for a minute."

"Why?"

"Because I want to kiss you," he answered bluntly.

Naomi went numb. "What?"

"Naomi, I know we've been friends for a long time, but I think the Lord is leading me in a new direction now. Would you mind if I courted you, officially?"

Naomi began to laugh, not knowing why.

Luke was not sure how to take her reaction. This was not the intimate scene he had envisioned.

Naomi reached out to touch his arm. "I'm sorry, Luke. I don't know why I'm laughing, really."

"I don't either. I'm trying to be serious." he was getting a little annoyed.

Naomi tried to control herself. In the near darkness of the shadow from the giant tree, she turned toward him. "Luke, if you are serious, then my answer is yes."

"Yes, you would mind?" he asked, beginning to doubt his grandfather's advice.

"No! I mean, yes, you can court me, officially."

Luke smiled, reaching for her arms. He pulled her close, kissing the lips he had been watching for weeks now.

Naomi's legs went numb, as she always thought they would. Her dreams were coming true. Her prayers were finally being answered. God had heard! He had seen all her tears. As pure joy swept through her body, Naomi accepted the future Christ Jesus had planned for her so long ago. In the back of her mind, she could only praise Him. "Thank you, Lord, thank you."

June sixteenth, 1884

"How was Chicago?" Betsy asked Naomi as they visited in the parlor of the Broderick estate.

"Wonderful. Simply wonderful," Naomi answered. "Your brother took me to three plays and a concert. We sailed on a boat across the lake and shopped for my trousseau. We saw all the pretty fountains and rode on the street cars. We even saw a telephone! It was just the best wedding trip a girl could ever wish for. Much the same as yours, I'm certain."

Both young brides shared stories. Betsy marveled at the wonders of traveling to and staying in San Francisco with her new husband. She spoke of the mountains and all their beauty, of the wonderful valleys in California and the exciting life in the city. She spoke fondly of the Pacific Ocean and its vast blue waters and rocky cliffs.

Naomi spoke of her new clothing: the lovely satin sleeping gowns, the seven pretty new dresses in wonderful colors trimmed with lace and ribbons, two new pairs of shoes and three new bonnets, petticoats and stockings and gloves and more. Such lovely things Luke had bought for her in Chicago. She was a real lady now.

Naomi could hardly wait to write her mother a letter telling her about the wonderful trip she had just taken. Both her parents had been so proud of her at the wedding. They had brought the entire family up from the farm to see their oldest daughter marry on her seventeenth birthday. It had been such a wonderful day, for everyone. The Lord was going to bless them indeed.

"And Betsy, I have to tell you, I had the strangest dream last night," Naomi looked around to make sure no one else was listening. "I dreamed that you and Jimmy had four children, all girls. Can you believe it? And he coming from a family of all boys?" After Betsy finished giggling, Naomi continued, "And Luke and I had five children. A boy, then a girl, then another boy, another girl and finally a boy."

"Do you think it will come true?" Betsy asked, thinking how fine their future would be.

Naomi tilted her head. "Only God knows, but wouldn't it be wonderful?"

"We are all going to be just wonderfully happy, I'm sure no matter what," Betsy stated. "God always looks out for our families."

Both young women agreed.

"By the way, you were right that night that I asked you about marrying Jimmy. Do you remember what you said? You told me as long as we used the money for good, that it would be good to marry him. Well, I just found out last week that he matched the funds the church raised last year at the bazaar!"

"That's wonderful! I'm so glad. And Luke told me he wants us to head up the campaign to collect blankets for the orphanage,"

Naomi added. "He's ordered a dozen from St. Louis already to add to what we will collect."

Betsy nodded. "You see? God looks out for us and lets us give back to His family. How blessed we are."

Naomi thought of all her prayers that had been answered over the last year. She nodded with Betsy. "How blessed we are indeed."

A Father's Prayer

Denver, Colorado
February, 1894

Gabriel sat still in his big chair. A warm fire blazed high in the brick fireplace. Even with a thick quilt on, he had a chill. At seventy-four, his body was having a hard time staying warm in the frigid Denver winter. With acceptance, he realized this might be his last year on earth. Since Gabriel Davidson had the peace of God in him, he knew this body on earth was temporary anyway. Soon, he would be going to his real home to walk the streets of gold with Christ and all those who had left before him. He would see his parents again. What a joy that would be. They had been gone now for so long, over thirty years.

Gabriel closed his eyes and thought back over his life. It had been good, mostly. There were many blessings and only one regret. His daughter, Missy, had not been heard from in over eighteen years. He did not even know if she was still alive. As a young woman, she had run off to marry a man inclined to drinking and gambling. Gabriel had tried to stop her, but she had married regardless of her father's advice and warnings. Roger had not provided well, moving himself, Missy, and their three children around frequently from town to town. In seventy-six, when Gabriel's three grandchildren left their parents to come live with him in Denver, Missy and Roger were in Dodge City. Gabriel wondered if she might still be there. He also wondered why Missy had never tried to contact her children in all these years. Luke was thirty-three now. He had been married for ten years and had five children with his wife, Naomi. They lived in a new large Victorian-style home about a mile away. Betsy was twenty-eight. She and her husband had four lovely daughters. Their son had died in infancy from pneumonia. It had been a dark time for their family, but relying on God's strength and grace, they had come through it. Betsy lived in an old grand estate, her husband's family home. They were quite well invested with the railroad that her husband managed. The last sibling was Steven. He was twenty-five. He and his wife, Fanny, had a new baby boy, just six months old named Adam. Steven and Fanny lived with Gabriel and his wife, Margaret, in the home Gabriel had lived in for forty years. It was a large two-story log home on a busy city street in Denver. The large room attached to the home that used to be the family store, was now remodeled into more rooms. It was more than enough space for five people to live very comfortably. When Luke took over running the business ten years ago, he had expanded their inventory and service. In time, their family mercantile had grown into a large department store, now housed in a new two-story brick building several blocks away. Luke and Steven managed the business very well. Gabriel was proud of all his grandchildren for their lives and accomplishments. His favorite part about it though, was they all believed in Jesus and worked to please the Lord in everything they did. Each family was active in the church, serving God and others. It was enough of a legacy to be proud of.

Margaret entered the parlor with two cups of hot steaming tea. "Gabriel, dear, are you awake?" she whispered. Her heavy blue grosgrain skirt rustled as she walked across the floor.

Gabriel looked at his white-haired wife. She stooped over a bit, and her skin showed signs of aging, but she was lovely still. "Yes."

"Fanny made us some tea. I added plenty of sugar to yours. Here, it will warm you."

Gabriel adjusted the blanket so he could take the saucer. "Thank you, dear."

"May I join you?" she asked.

"Please do. I was just resting," he answered.

Margaret was Gabriel's second wife. His first, the mother of Missy, had died decades ago when Missy was fourteen. He had had a good second marriage with Margaret. She was a fine bred lady, always careful with her speech and her appearance. She brought him honor by all the work she did helping others. Margaret had been a wonderful step-grandmother to his three grandchildren, helping him raise them in a respectable home. She was a blessing to them all indeed.

"You know, dear, I've been sitting here thinking about my life and it has been very good."

She gave him a smile.

"I thank God for sending you to me years ago. You've been a wonderful wife."

Margaret leaned over and patted him on the hand. "Thank you, honey."

"I'm blessed by everyone around me, all my family," he continued. "But there is one thing that is still unsettled. I'm thinking maybe God is keeping me here in this tired old body because I still have one more thing to do."

"What's that?" Margaret asked in a quiet voice.

"I need to find Missy."

Margaret nodded.

"When Steven gets home tonight I'm going to speak with him about it. I want to find her, bring her back into the family. She's been my wayward daughter, like the prodigal son in the Bible. I want to bring her back and be reunited." Small tears slid from his eyes and down his cheeks.

Margaret held her husband's hand as her heart squeezed in pain for him. "I'm sure Steven and Luke will find her. I'm sure they would like to see their mother again. It's been so long."

Gabriel stared into the fire. "Please, Lord. Let me find her," he prayed.

Luke and Steven were looking over the sums in their accounting books in their joint office upstairs at the department store. Eight employees were working diligently at their stations, helping customers. Naomi's brother, Johnathan, worked on the bottom floor managing the grocery department. At twenty-three years old, he was turning out to be quite a business man.

Luke was speaking with Steven about possibly hiring another employee when someone tapped on their office door.

"Come in," Luke answered.

Both brothers looked up. Johnathan entered the room carrying a piece of paper.

"It's a telegram for you, Mister Carter," he said, handing it to Steven.

"Thank you, Johnathan," he answered. The young man left the room, closing the door behind him.

"It's from a detective agency," Steven told Luke. He read it out loud. "*Found Missy Carter in Guthrie, Oklahoma. Walker's Saloon. Please advise.*"

The brothers exchanged glances. "She's working in a saloon?" Steven stated out loud what they both were thinking. All sorts of imaginings swept through their minds.

"We have to go get her," Luke stated.

"I wonder how Grandfather will take this news," Steven added. He walked over to the telephone mounted to the wall. After speaking with the operator, he waited for his wife to answer at home.

"Fanny, I just received a telegram from the detective agency. Please tell my grandfather that my mother was found in Guthrie. Luke and I are making plans to go get her. Yes. Thank you, dear. Bye," he said, hanging up the receiver.

Luke was putting on his coat to walk down to the train station. He wanted to get tickets for the journey.

Steven was deep in thought. "You know, brother, we really shouldn't both go. One of us needs to stay here and run the store. I'll stay if you want me to, but you know more than I do and, really, you're in charge. Plus you have five children at home. I've only the one. It would be easier for me to go."

Luke thought about what he said. It was true. One of them did need to stay behind. "You are right. As much as I would like to go with you, we both can't leave at the same time."

"I'll go get my ticket," Steven told him, "and go home to speak with Grandfather. Was there anything else I needed to do here today?"

"Not really. Nothing that can't wait. Mother is more important right now," Luke agreed.

Bracing himself for the freezing air, Steven wrapped up in his coat, hat, gloves and scarf. "I will call you at home tonight to let you know what my plans are."

"I might stop by the house later," Luke told him.

"See you then."

The next morning, Steven left on the six o'clock train to Kansas. He would head east first, hoping the train could push through any snowdrifts over the tracks. After spending the night in Wichita, he would head south into Oklahoma. He had promised to send a wire letting the family know the day of his return. Grandfather had given him five hundred dollars. This was to be given to Missy regardless of whether she came back with him or not. It was Gabriel's gift to let his daughter know he still cared. There was no bitterness in his heart, only sorrow over the many years wasted. He had been devastated to find out she was working in a saloon. How very far she had gone from God.

The day was clear and sunny when Steven stepped onto the wooden platform in Guthrie. The bright blue sky was a stark contrast to the mottled mix of snow, dead grass and paprika colored clay covering the ground. The coldness of the air, however, could be seen with every breath. Swirls of vapor came from every man, woman, child and animal. But the sun in the south with it's bright glow warmed Steven's heart with courage. "Lord, please let my mother be open to me," he prayed. "Let this bright sunshine be a sign from you that all will be well."

In his fine suit, hat and warm coat, Steven asked a nearby colored attendant, "Can you tell me how to get to the Walker Saloon?"

The black man gave him a strange look, but pointed to the left. "Go down that way fo' blocks, then turn north. You'll see it."

"Thank you," Steven told him, tipping his hat.

Carrying his only satchel, Steven began the walk toward his mother. He concentrated on his heartbeat. He wanted to keep it steady, keep his breathing steady, or his nerves would get the best of him. He spotted a nice looking hotel, three stories with red brick and curtains in every window. Going inside, he paid for a room. At least he would have good accommodations tonight. And there was a restaurant across the street. It would soon be supper time. Maybe he could convince his mother to eat with him. He was trying to remember what she looked like. He had only been seven when Luke took him away to live with Grandfather. Apparently, that had been a good decision on his brother's part. Steven wondered where he and his siblings would be today if they had not run away to the safety of Gabriel's Christian home.

Steven deposited his bag in the room and left for the saloon. He found the rundown building in a poor part of town. There was broken glass on the porch. Shutters were hanging from rusted out hinges on the upstairs windows. The side alley smelled of beer and urine. Steven cringed. This place was filthy.

He stepped inside. All eyes turned toward him. He was out of place in his fine clean and tailored clothes. As a dozen men stared, the stench of body odor seeped up his nose. He let out a cough, covering his mouth and nose. His eyes scanned the room, looking for a female that resembled his mother. She was not there.

Steven stepped up to the bar. "I'm looking for Missy Carter," he told the man behind the counter.

Grease from his last meal still clung to the scruffy beard of the bartender. He narrowed his eyes. "Who's askin'? You the law or somethin'?" he said with a mouth missing several teeth.

"No. Tell her Steven Carter is looking for her."

"Steven Carter?" The bartender looked Steven up and down suspiciously. "You kin?"

"That's business between us," Steven answered, wishing he had not forgotten his pocket knife back in the hotel room. This man and the crowd in the room looked capable of violence.

Spitting a little tobacco juice onto the floor, the dirty man turned and pulled on a cord behind the bar. "She'll be down in a minute," he answered. "Want a drink?"

Steven shook his head. "No, thank you." Instead, he stood and waited.

When he heard footsteps coming down the stairs, he looked toward it. A dull red skirt came into the view. Then his mother appeared. Old and worn-looking, with silver streaks of unruly hair. The top of her dress scooped low, showing too much neck and skin. In his heart, he was ashamed.

She looked at the bartender, then back at the young man. "What do you want?" she asked.

"A word with you, please," Steven told her.

"I ain't broke no laws," she defended herself.

"I'm not the law," Steven assured her.

"Says his name is Steven Carter," the greasy man spoke.

Missy stopped in her tracks and stared wide-eyed. "Steven?" she choked out. He nodded. Missy braced herself with a chair. She sat in it slowly. "Steve," she said again, still hardly believing it was her youngest son, after all this time.

Steven walked over to his mother. "Can we talk for a while?" he asked. She nodded toward another chair at the table. He sat down. "We only learned of your whereabouts three days ago. Grandfather was pleased to learn you were still alive."

"He's still alive?" she asked. He would be in his seventies now.

"Yes. Alive, but very old and weak. He wants to see you again before he dies. That is why he had Luke and me find you," Steven explained.

"How is Luke?" she asked casually.

"He's fine. He has a wife and five children. We still run the store, but it's much bigger now."

"I can see you are doing well," Missy responded.

"Betsy is well, too. She married well. They have four daughters. And my wife just had a son six months ago. That makes ten grandchildren you have."

Missy laughed in spite of herself. "My," she answered.

"Where is father? Is he still here?" Steven asked.

Missy shook her head. "Killed eight years ago. Shot in the street. Gunfight."

"Hmm," Steven replied. It did not surprise him.

"And have you been here all this time?" Steven asked. "Why didn't you come home to Denver?"

Missy shook her head and looked away. "I've been here ten years. And I won't never go back to Denver."

"Why not? A lot of people are hoping you will," he told her.

"Why? So my father can say how right he was? So he can rub it in my face that I've had an awful life? So he can tell me what trash I am, how ashamed he is of me? I don't think so."

Steven sat back in his chair. "Lord, give me the words," he said under his breath. "No, Mother. Grandfather wants to tell you that he still loves you. He wants to see you again before he dies. He wants to know that you are happy before he leaves you."

Missy was doubtful.

"Mother, let me take you out of this place. It's filthy. You don't belong here. You were made for more than this. I've a room all prepared for you at home. My wife is fixing it right now, as we speak. Luke and Betsy are anxious to see you, too. Wouldn't you like to see your grandchildren?"

Missy looked down at the floor. She said nothing.

After an awkward silence, Steven continued, "You don't like living here, do you?"

Missy took a deep breath and looked Steven in the eye. "Go home, Steven. Go home to your grandfather. Go home to your wife and your child. Have a good life." With those words, his mother stood from the table. "Goodbye, Steven," she spoke.

Steven watched in disbelief as his mother walked back up the stairs. He could not believe what she had just said. Was her heart that hardened by all these years? He wanted to save her from this place, save her from herself. Her own pride was keeping her from the love of her family. From the love of her father.

On the walk to his hotel, Steven determined not to give up. He would try again tomorrow. Besides, there was the money to give to his mother. Remembering the sorry state of her dress, he walked into the mercantile. He bought soap and wash cloths, new petticoats and drawers, a basic corset, a camisole and stockings. From the rack of pre-sewn clothing, he chose a lady's modest black dress made from heavy cotton. It was adorned with petite white lace ruffles sewn along the seams. He also chose a silvery-green two-piece dress and a white blouse that could be worn with it. Lastly, he found a warm bonnet, a pair of gloves, a pair of shoes and a dark blue chenille cape. It was soft and warm. He put all these items in a new satchel. The clerk was more than delighted to make the sale, telling Steven to "please come again."

Steven dropped the goods off in his hotel room and went to eat across the street. He spent much time in deep thought about the whole encounter this afternoon. That night in his room, he spent much time in prayer. "Dear Jesus, help my mother to see we are only trying to help. God, only you can change this bitterness and pride in her heart. Help me to know what to say tomorrow when I go back. Jesus, she needs to be redeemed. Help her, help her. Amen."

Steven returned at ten the next day. His mother was sitting on a stool at the bar, drinking a shot of whiskey. Her dress today was a tattered blue gown at least two decades old.

"What are you doing back here?" she asked him. "I thought I told you to go home."

"You did," Steven answered. "And I will, just not yet. I have something to give you."

She looked at him with a smirk. "What? More holier than thou advice?" The bartender laughed.

Steven shot him an ugly look. "No. This is for you," he said, placing the satchel on the bar. "Don't open it until I leave. And I advise you to do it in private, in your room."

Missy raised her eyebrows. "What is it?"

"A gift. From me and Grandfather."

"I don't want nothing from him," she answered.

Steven tipped his hat. "Goodbye, Mother," he said out loud for the bartender to hear. "I'll give everyone your best regards and let them know you couldn't make it because you had to work." Steven could see his mother was getting riled. "I'll write to you. Take care."

"Now see here!" she said loudly, putting defiant hands on her hips.

"Good day!" Steven said before she could go on. He left the nasty saloon with haste. "Lord, I hope that works!" he said out loud to the sky. "It's what I felt you telling me to do, so I did it."

Steven spent the rest of the day reading in the parlor of the hotel. He found several newspapers, not more than a week old. It was interesting reading from St. Louis, Memphis, Dallas, even Santa Fe. He tried not to think too much about his mother.

Steven did think about it though the next morning as he dressed to leave. He wondered if his mother had gone through the bag. He wondered if she had found the envelope with five hundred dollars and a one way train ticket to Denver. He also wondered if she would show up this morning at the train station. He doubted it. Grabbing his satchel, he left. Steven went across the street for breakfast. He ate steak and eggs, two biscuits with jam and washed it down with both a large glass of milk and a cup of coffee. The train left at nine. He had thirty minutes to go. Just enough time to send a telegraph home.

Steven sat patiently in the station. There were two dozen other people waiting to board. The train from Oklahoma city was waiting in the station. When the foreman blew his whistle, he stood from the bench, taking his bag with him. After ten minutes, he and the other passengers were settled into one of the two passenger cars. He sat across from another man dressed in similar attire. Behind him, were two cowboys. Also in the car was a family with six children. They were quite noisy. A pretty young woman with her colored maid sat in the very back. Steven looked out the window one last time at Guthrie. He noticed the ice house sitting not far from the station with big red letters when someone else boarded the train. He turned to see who it was. His mother, wearing the new silver-green dress, stared right in his face. Her eyes were red and swollen, but she was there. He stood immediately.

"Mother!" he said with surprise.

Her eyes showed pain, inner pain and turmoil. "Steven."

"Here, let me take your bag," he offered.

Missy settled herself on the bench beside her son. Steven's heart was pounding, as he was sure, hers was as well. He did not dare ask why she had changed her mind. He could already tell she had been crying. He gave her a smile. "The conductor said we should have good weather," Steven told her. "We should be in Wichita well before supper."

She smiled and nodded.

"Did you have time to eat this morning?" he asked.

"No."

"Want me to get you something?" he wondered.

"No."

He then realized she was probably too nervous and upset to eat. "Well, we'll have a good supper tonight. The hotel in Wichita is very nice."

Steven and his mother made small talk for the next hour. Nothing really significant was spoken. After a short silence, he noticed she was crying again. He offered his handkerchief. She took it thankfully. "Keep it," he told her. He had half a dozen more just like it at home.

Finally, Missy asked for information. "So, tell me about everyone again."

Two hours were taken up discussing the family. Steven went over the names again of spouses and children. He knew it would take her a while to learn them all. He told her all about the new department store, and of the changes they made to the old store, turning it into a new kitchen and parlor. "And you won't recognize Denver. It's changed so much. Over one hundred thousand people live there now."

"That is hard to believe."

"Believe it. There is much to do and see," he assured her.

"When I grew up there, it was just a busy western town. Full of mountain men, soldiers, Indian scouts, a few pioneers and a few business men," she told him. "I wonder if any of my childhood friends are still there."

"Who were they?"

"Cindy McNally, Sarah Sinclair, Beverly Howard," she answered.

"I think Nattie has a mother named Sarah," Steven told her. "Nattie is one of Betsy's friends. That might be her."

"It would be nice to see them after all this time. But they know what I did. How can I ever show my face to them again?" Missy asked, not really expecting an answer.

After a moment's thought, Steven replied, "People change, Mother. Today you are a new you, different from the person you were yesterday."

Missy forced a weak smile. She cried quietly again for some time.

Late that afternoon in Wichita, Steven arranged for two rooms and a private bath for his mother. She bathed before going to supper and came out in the same green dress. This time, however, her hair was braided neatly and pinned on her head. Her eyes were still framed below with dark circles, but some of the swelling around them was gone.

"You look nice," he complimented.

She let out a little chuckle. It had been a long time since a proper gentleman had given her a kind word.

"Do you want to wear your gloves?" he asked.

"Is the dining room that formal?"

Steven nodded.

Missy took the white gloves he had given her and pulled them onto her hands. She took Steven's arm that he offered to escort her downstairs.

"Don't be nervous," he assured her. "It's just supper."

They ate a fine meal of fried fish, baked apples, potatoes, green beans and rolls. They enjoyed light conversation about the hotel and restaurant and the people passing by. Missy was very self-conscious. Her clothing made her look the part, but she knew the lady inside her was long forgotten. She made every effort to watch her manners and mimic the movements of other ladies in the room.

Toward the end of the meal, she looked at her son. "Steven you make me very proud of you. You are a fine gentleman, I can tell. Your black suit is very becoming and your character is just as becoming."

Surprised by her declaration, Steven answered, "Thank you."

The next morning at breakfast, Missy confessed, "I've not slept so well in years as I did last night. That bed was so comfortable and warm."

Steven was pleased. He had thought for sure she would have tossed and turned last night with nervousness. Maybe she was getting more comfortable with the idea of going home. He had spent half an hour last night praying about it.

They both ordered waffles and sausage. Thick maple syrup made them taste delicious. It was a hearty meal before the long ride home. Steven ordered some extra fruit and bread for the trip as well.

When the train pulled out at seven-twenty, Missy's nerves began to tense.

"How long until we get there?" she asked.

"It's an all day trip. I sent a telegram this morning from the hotel. They will be expecting us tonight."

It was a long day. The train had to stop twice in Colorado while snow was cleared from the tracks. The sky had clouded up again as well. It was possible, more snow was on the way. Missy's anxiety grew by the hour. She knew they would all be judging her. Several times she regretted coming. She did not really know why she had come. Something had just made her do it, but she was now condemning herself over and over.

Finally they arrived. Snow flurries were just beginning to fall. A cold wind blew them in from the north. Missy was grateful for the warm dress and soft warm cape. She retied the bow on her bonnet, securing it to her head. Steven helped her off the train. Missy gulped as she recognized her oldest son, Luke, heading their way.

"Mama," he called out, embracing her. Missy was greatly surprised. She had not expected a warm reception.

"Luke," she answered back, patting him.

"Mama, it is good to see you. You look well," he said, taking her gloved hand. "Come, I've a nice warm carriage waiting. And there's a warm meal back at the house," Luke turned to his brother. "Why was the train so late?"

"Snow drifts. They had to stop and clear the way," Steven told him.

Steven carried the two satchels to the carriage and climbed in with his mother and brother. The driver led them home to Gabriel's house.

"I was getting worried. There's a bad snowstorm on the way. White out conditions already in Cheyenne and west of here," Luke told them.

"Is everyone at the house?" Steven asked.

"Margaret is planning a big meal tomorrow afternoon for the whole family. Betsy and Jimmy will come in the morning, and Naomi and the children are still at home. They knew you would be getting in late and wanted Grandfather to have some time with Mother by himself," Luke told them. "But with this weather like it is, who knows?"

"Are you going back home tonight?" Missy asked.

"Don't know. Doesn't look like I will be able to," Luke answered.

After a few short minutes, the carriage stopped. Missy looked out the window. The home looked the same on the outside. She swallowed the lump in her throat. She felt as though she might be sick.

Steven brought his mother up the steps and into the doorway. Luke followed behind with the bags after paying the hired driver for his services. Margaret and Gabriel heard the commotion from the parlor.

"They are here," Fanny announced.

When Gabriel rounded the doorway and caught sight of his only child, tears spilled freely from his eyes. "Missy, my dear Missy!" he wailed, opening his arms for an embrace. He moved his tired body in her direction. She, too, began to weep, stepping into his arms after three decades. Gabriel was sobbing loudly. He stroked Missy's back. "You're home, you're home," he repeated over and over. "Thank you, sweet Jesus!"

There was not a dry eye in the room. Everyone wept over the reunion. Luke was reminded of the reunion in the Bible between Joseph and his many brothers in Egypt. He remembered how Joseph had wept. His father now was relieving himself of all the pain thirty-three years had wrought. Pain and sorrow of a lost daughter finally returning home. Luke pulled a handkerchief from his pocket.

After much weeping and embracing, Missy was led to the dining room. Fanny brought in a succulent ham, roasted to perfection with sweet juices. Since it was nine o'clock, the rest of the family had already eaten, but Missy and Steven helped themselves to the wonderful meal. Buttered rice and boiled cabbage were brought out as well.

Gabriel could not keep from staring at his daughter. There were dark circles underneath her eyes. He wondered how she had fared these last twenty years since he last heard of her in Dodge City. It would be interesting to see how these next few days would go. In his heart, he praised the Lord for bringing his child home.

Fanny held baby Adam at the breakfast table the next morning. Steven and Luke sat nearby eating their pancakes and fried ham. The rest of the house was still asleep. They had stayed up rather late last night talking in the parlor. Luke had called home letting Naomi know he would be spending the night. With the snowstorm as it was, travel was too risky at night. It had blown over in the dark, now the bright sunshine gleamed off freshly fallen snow. It brought bright light into the dining room.

"That saloon in Guthrie was deplorable. I wouldn't want my dog living there," Steven told them. "I praise God for Mother coming back with me. I didn't think she would."

"I'm glad she did, too. The sooner we get her settled in here, the better," Luke agreed.

"Steven, I noticed your mother only had the one bag when you came in last night. Is that all she owns?" Fanny asked.

He nodded. "Yes. I bought her some new clothes in Guthrie, just two dresses and some underthings though. Shoes, the cape and a hat. That's all she has."

"Two won't do at all," Fanny decided, shaking her head. "We will just have to see that she gets some more clothing right away."

"We have quite a bit in stock at the store, if you want to bring her down later," Luke suggested.

"Are you going in today?" Fanny asked of her husband and brother-in-law.

"Yes, but we will be back early for the big dinner Margaret has planned," Steven answered.

A short time later, the men left for the department store. Fanny entertained Adam in the parlor reading him a book, but he was more interested in picking at the silk pleats on the bodice of her gray-lavender dress. By nine o'clock Margaret and Gabriel made it downstairs for a late breakfast. The cook left it warming on the stove while she prepared for tonight's big meal.

Fanny joined them at the dining table. "How did it go last night?" she asked. She and Steven had gone to bed before them.

"It went will," Gabriel told her. "We made amends, after all this time. I think she will stay here. I can only pray she will be happy again."

"She will. We'll see to it," Margaret assured him with a secret pat on his leg underneath the table.

Missy Carter opened her eyes after a wonderful night of sleep. At first, she did not recognize the room, but then remembered she was home. Last night had been good. Better than she had ever dreamed it would go. Her father had been kind and loving, embracing her without question or judgment. He had said nothing to make her feel guilty about the poor choices she had made in life. Tears began to flow again. It was hard to understand that kind of love. Missy had gone without it for so very, very long. Even she had been a poor kind of mother, not loving her children enough. The best thing she had ever done was let them leave. She had a lot of years of making up to do, if they would let her. Oh, how sorry she was for everything.

Sitting up in the warm bed, Missy took a deep breath. "Lord, I am so sorry." A sob broke out. "Please forgive me for everything. I've been so bad." Tears fell silently. "I believed on you when I was a child. I know you saved me then. I went so far away from you though, doing what I wanted. Help me to have that faith again like I did when I was eight. I need it, Jesus. I need you." Missy wiped away some of the tears with her battered old nightgown. "I know I'm old. Fifty-two is old, but I know it's not too late to change. Please help me. I haven't spoken to you for so long, but please hear me now, Jesus. I'm sorry. I'm sorry for everything."

Missy fell back against the covers and cried into her pillow. All the heartache of the hard life she had chosen for herself came out. When Missy stopped crying, she felt as though a weight had been lifted from her chest. She felt so much better. Knowing it must be late in the morning, she resolved to go downstairs and change her life. Picking up the black dress with leg-of-mutton sleeves and white lace trim along the bodice and shoulders, she dressed. She pulled her hair into a simple bun, pinning it securely. Taking a small cloth by the wash basin, Missy patted cool water on her face, trying to soothe the burn in her eyes. After a few more deep breaths, she left the room and headed downstairs. She found her father, Margaret, Fanny and baby Adam, in the dining room at the table.

"Good morning," Margaret greeted first.

Missy nodded to them all with a little smile.

"Yes, come in Missy. Get some coffee and join us for breakfast," Gabriel suggested. "I was just reading a letter I received yesterday from a friend. His name is Isaac Martin. He lives close to Naomi's parents."

Dear Davidsons,

All is well on our homestead. Opal and I and the boys are enjoying some rest this winter. We are reading through the books you sent for Christmas, and thank you for that wonderful gift. Abel especially likes the sea adventures. Aaron enjoys the science and biology studies. Andrew acts out some of the plays for us, and keeps us entertained.

Opal has requested I bring our entire family into Denver this summer, so I will do so to keep them all happy. We will come and visit you again, of course, and hope to attend your church as well. Opal and I truly enjoyed the choir singing last time we came. The woman is more spiritual than I am. Can you imagine that? God is good!

We had a visit from Chad and Helen Jenkins recently. Their son, Michael, is getting married this spring. They have asked for my help with a new cabin. I'm sure Naomi has told you all about it. Everyone is growing up so quickly. Even the Jenkins twins are young adults now. I'm feeling old!

Rest easy this winter, and we will see you in a few months.

Your friend, Isaac Martin.

"That's a good letter," Margaret smiled. She turned to Missy who now sat drinking coffee. "Care for some breakfast?"

"Yes, please."

Gabriel stood. "I will get it."

When he walked into the kitchen, Margaret turned to her husband's daughter. "He's so glad you're here. You have no idea.

Tonight's supper is very important. I planned on serving roast beef. Does that suit you?"

"Fine, thank you," Missy answered. She was a little self-conscious with everyone being so nice. Her father's new wife seemed very kind, but Missy still felt a little awkward about the new relationship.

"Good. Everyone will be here by four. But cook has it all under control so our day is free. The storm is gone, so we can go to the store if you like," Margaret suggested.

She nodded slightly. "Where are Luke and Steven this morning?" Missy asked.

"They are already at work," Fanny answered. "They left at eight."

"What time is it?"

"I think about nine-thirty," Gabriel answered, returning with the loaded tray.

"Thank you, Father," Missy told him, thankful for the food.

"So, what have you women decided to do today?" he asked cheerfully.

Margaret turned to him, "I think we are going to go see the department store."

"Oh, good. I'd like to go, too."

By eleven, they were on their way, riding in a closed carriage. Missy had one hundred dollars in her glove. She wanted a new nightgown and anything else she might need to live in a proper home once again. Maybe some house slippers too, so she would not have to wear the black ones constantly.

Missy peeked out the window of the carriage. The town had transformed itself over the years. She hardly recognized anything. Tall buildings had sprung up where little wooden shacks had once stood. The horses stopped in front of a brick building with a wide porch and steps.

"Here we are," Margaret announced.

Gabriel helped them all down from the little step and ushered them inside where it would be warm. "While you ladies look around," he said, "I'll just go up and let the boys know we're here."

"I can't believe this is Papa's store," Missy spoke out loud looking around at all the merchandise.

"Your sons have done well with it," Margaret agreed.

"Where to first?" Fanny asked. She was eager to look around as well. Adam was home taking a morning nap while Cora looked after him in between her chores in the kitchen.

"I brought some money Father gave me. I want to look at night clothes," she told them. The women headed upstairs where the women's clothing was located.

After two hours shopping and half an hour visiting with Steven and Luke, the family group left the store. Missy carried numerous packages, including the new house shoes she wanted. When the carriage reached home, a warm soup was waiting for them. After lunch, Margaret and Gabriel excused themselves for their afternoon nap. Fanny and Missy were left to themselves.

"I really like the dresses you picked out," Fanny told her.

"Thank you. It's been such a long time since I've had nice clothes to wear," she told her. "Steven bought me two dresses in Guthrie. Those are the only two I brought with me."

"They are pretty. He has good taste, doesn't he?"

Missy smiled with a little laugh. "I guess he does."

"I think it comes from being in the department store business. He has to know what women like so the clothes will sell," Fanny explained.

"Where does he get it all from?" Missy wondered.

"Some of it is made here, but a lot of it is shipped out from back East. He orders most of it from companies in St. Louis, Chicago, and New York.

"My goodness!"

"Well, everyone will be here in less than two hours. Did Steven give you all the names of everyone?" Fanny asked.

"Yes, but I know I won't remember them all."

"What if I wrote them down, would that help?" the younger woman suggested.

"Yes."

Handing off Adam to her mother-in-law, Fanny walked over to a nearby desk and pulled out pen and paper. She wrote out a chart for Missy to study. Luke married Naomi and they have five children: Benjamin 9, Suellen 7, Timothy 6, Maggie 4, Bo Johnathan 2. Betsy married James Broderick. Their children are Ruby Lynn 9, Lydia Mae 8, Olive Rose 5, and Bonnie Jo 4.

"Here, this should help."

Missy handed back the warm little boy to his mother. She read over the paper. "I might go upstairs and study this for a while before I get ready. Do you mind?"

"No, please do. I need to freshen up myself and little Adam here needs to be changed," Fanny answered.

Needing a little time to herself, Missy went upstairs.

The telephone rang at four o'clock. Luke and Naomi were running late, but they were leaving their house in five minutes. Missy came down in her new blue suit. She felt like such a new woman, all cleaned up inside and out. Margaret wore a stunning lavender gown. Fanny had on a dull red dress, accented by pretty lace at the neck. The men wore dark suits. Missy's stomach was in knots as they waited in the parlor for everyone to arrive.

"Just think how noisy this house is going to be in a few short minutes," Steven joked with them all.

Finally, Betsy arrived with her husband and daughters.

"Oh, Mama!" she shouted, running out of the carriage. They embraced fondly on the front porch.

"Hello, baby," Missy answered with a lump in her throat. Her daughter was lovely, absolutely lovely. Her pale blue heavy silk gown peeked out beneath the warm brown coat trimmed with seal fur. "You look so good."

"Thank you, Mama. You do, too. It's been so long," Betsy cried.

"Yes, far too long. And I'm sorry for that," she said, tears beginning to sting her eyes. "But I can tell that Margaret was a good mother to you."

Betsy smiled, giving Margaret a glance.

"Come in out of this cold, everyone," Gabriel encouraged.

Betsy's husband, tall with dark hair, helped their four daughters from the carriage. Each one wore a red tweed coat with hood. They were adorable. Once inside, Betsy introduced them all. Missy embraced each one, enjoying the feel of her granddaughters. They all gave her a smile.

"I made you this," Ruby Lynn told her, handing out a sheet of paper. "It's a picture of our house. I drew it at school."

"Thank you, it's very nice," Missy told her, looking at the sheet.

Lydia Mae smiled, but stared. Missy wasn't sure what the girls had been told. She hoped they did not know the truth. Olive Rose went straight to Margaret, wanting to be picked up. Margaret held her hand instead. Bonnie Jo showed her the doll she carried. "Her name is Nellie," the four-year-old said.

"She's very nice," Missy announced.

"Shall we wait in the parlor for Luke and Naomi?" Margaret suggested. She turned to Betsy. "They called a few minutes ago and are running a little late. It seems Bo knocked over a vase of flowers on his sister's dress. It got all wet, so they had to change her."

Olive sat by Margaret while the other three girls stayed close to their mother.

"Betsy, your mother went by the store today," Gabriel started the conversation.

"Oh, what did you think? Isn't it grand?" Betsy asked.

Conversation centered around this subject for ten minutes until Luke and Naomi arrived.

In they came with all five children. Introductions were made again. Nine-year-old Benjamin offered his hand to Missy instead of a hug. It was endearing to say the least. He was more cautious. Suellen handed her a cut daffodil.

"Thank you, sweetie. I love flowers," Missy told her. "I will put this in a jar in my room."

The little girl smiled and walked back next to her mother.

"It is good to meet you," Naomi said, extending her hand as well.

Cora announced that dinner was ready. The entire family moved into the dining area. A small table and chairs was set up in a corner for the younger children. Their plates were served first after Gabriel prayed over the food.

"Thank you, sweet Jesus, for this family reunion. It is an answered prayer. You've made an old man happy. Please continue to help us do your will in this world until we come home to you. I ask a special blessing for Missy. May you keep her back in the arms of her family. We love you, Jesus. Bless this food to nourish us. Amen."

Two months passed. Missy settled into life in Denver with ease. She even attended church regularly with the family and helped Margaret with her volunteer work. She enjoyed the companionship of her children again and the pure joy her grandchildren brought. Spring was coming closer more and more each week, bringing much anticipated warmer weather. The family's Easter celebration was joyful as well. After church services, they gathered at Betsy's home for a large meal and games on the lawn.

A twenty by twenty foot pen was made from blocks of hay. James purchased ten rabbits, and put them loose inside. On the count of three, all the children except for Adam began chasing the one they wanted for their own. The girls giggled with delight. The boys shouted with eagerness as the rabbits tried to escape.

"Thanks a lot, James," Luke ribbed him. "Now I have to make cages so we don't have fifty rabbits running around our back yard."

The adults all chuckled. "It's for the children, Luke," James teased in return.

Later that afternoon, while the younger children slept and the older ones played outside, Missy spoke up, "Luke, do you think you and Steven could spare a small space in the store for a flower shop?"

"Really, Mother?"

She nodded.

"I'm sure we could. What do you have in mind?" Steven asked.

"Well, I was thinking how nice it would be to have one. I've always liked flowers," she answered.

"Your mother did, too," Gabriel added from his chair in the corner. He could feel his body trying to take a nap, but wanted to stay awake for the conversation.

"Did she? I don't remember that."

Gabriel smiled and nodded.

Missy told them about her plans. She still had four hundred dollars from the money her father had given her. She wanted to use one hundred for summer clothes, but the remaining money she hoped to invest in a small shop.

"Mother, there is a small space for rent across the street from the department store. Let me look into it. Our floor space is already wall to wall merchandise, so you might be better off in a room where you could grow," Steven suggested.

"Are you sure you want to work?" Luke asked her.

"Would it embarrass you if I did?" Missy asked. She had not thought of that. A working woman in the family might bring disgrace.

"Oh, no. If you want a flower shop then I think you should have one," Luke answered. "I just don't want you to have to miss time with your grandchildren."

Everyone else nodded.

Missy forced a smile and confessed the truth, "Well, I'm feeling bad about not contributing any way to the family's income. With Father's permission, I would like to try with this money."

The following week, Luke arranged to rent out the space. Missy ordered shelving from a local carpenter and contacted distributors for her inventory. She also ordered tissue paper, boxes, ribbons, vases and buckets from her son's department store. She also hired a painter to make a sign. "Flower Shoppe" it read in large red letters. As a surprise, Luke, Steven and Gabriel ordered a red-and-white-striped awning to be placed over the front of the store. It really stood out and drew attention to the new business.

In mid-May, Missy opened for business. Her father had not been feeling well for a few days and had to stay home during her grand opening. Everyone else in the family came though, admiring what she had done in the store. Even her grandchildren had fun smelling all the colorful flowers. She let them each choose one as a present. Her first day of business was busy and time passed swiftly. When she returned to the house at five that evening, her happiness of the day was shattered.

Margaret was upstairs tending her husband. Gabriel had developed a high fever during the afternoon. What they thought was just a summer head cold had developed into something else. He was having a hard time breathing.

"Oh no, not now!" Missy cried out in the hallway when Margaret told her. Everything was going just right in her life. She couldn't lose her father now.

"The doctor came by earlier today. There's not much that can be done. He's old and tired. I think his time is coming," Margaret said, large pools of water collecting in her eyes. "God, give me strength," she said out loud. Margaret walked back down the hallway to return to the kitchen for more cool rags.

Missy entered the room. Fanny sat in a chair, eyes red from crying. Steve too stood against the wall with watery eyes. "Have you told Betsy and Luke?" she asked.

Steve nodded.

"They are coming," Fanny answered.

Missy knelt down beside the bed and took her father's hand. "Papa, can you hear me?" she asked.

Gabriel nodded.

"Papa, I just want you to know that you were right. I'm so sorry I caused you so much sorrow."

She looked at his face as he squeezed her hand. A small tear slid down his right cheek.

"Thank you for letting me come back home. Thank you for loving me no matter how awful I was. I've asked God to forgive me too. You know, I recommitted to him that first morning I was here," she confessed, her chest tightening with emotion.

He squeezed her hand again as another tear slid down his face. "I love you, Father," she added.

Gabriel opened his eyes. "I love you, too," he spoke in labored words. "You were my last prayer, Missy. I asked God to bring you back home so I could see you before I died," he said softly. "I knew this was coming. Don't be sad for me."

Large tears slid from Missy's eyes as she held to her father's hand. She could not speak. "Tell everyone goodbye," he said. Gabriel closed his eyes. His breathing became more labored again.

Margaret returned with the cloth. She saw everyone crying and looked at Gabriel's still form on the bed. Her throat closed in fear.

"Margaret," Gabriel whispered.

Taking another breath of relief, she walked quickly to the bed. "Yes, I'm here," she said.

Gabriel held out his other hand for her to take. She slid her fingers in his. "I'm not afraid," he managed. "Be brave for me. God is here." More labored breaths. He then pulled his arms together to put Missy's hand in Margaret's. "Mother and daughter," he spoke quietly. "Goodbye, Margaret, my love."

Gabriel released their hands, dropping his own onto his stomach. They all watched in sadness as he took his last few breaths. When the labored breathing stopped, Margaret's head fell against the mattress. She cried for the love of her life who was gone. He who was so full of life, so full of love for God and all those around him. She heard Missy crying, too. They still held hands, knowing they were drawing strength together.

"God, help me get through this," Margaret prayed quietly. "I know he's with you now. I know he's happy. Give me courage. I'll miss him so much." tears broke her thoughts.

Steven placed a hand on Margaret's shoulder. Fanny comforted Missy. A part of them all was gone, but they had so much to remember him by. So many good memories, and the peace of God. Because of Gabriel and his belief in Jesus, they would all meet again in heaven. He had shared it with them all, his wife, his three grandchildren, their spouses. And all the grandchildren would grow up to know Christ as their savior as well. It was a legacy anyone could be proud of. Generations to come would follow in his footsteps. Luke and Naomi's middle son, Timothy, would go into the mission field, traveling to Indo-China, preaching the word of Christ to thousands. Betsy and Jimmy's daughter, Olive Rose, would go into nursing, witnessing to hundreds of wounded soldiers during the First World War. Steven and Fanny's firstborn son, Adam, would grow up to become a preacher, saving thousands during the Great Depression.

Missy Davidson Carter died at an old age of ninety in nineteen thirty-two. Her granddaughters, Suellen and Maggie, took over the flower shop. She went there five days a week until she was eighty-five and unable to get around as easily. She continued to live with Steven and Fanny until their sixth child was born in nineteen-o-two. Missy then moved in with Betsy and Jimmy in their large family estate. Missy grew close to her three children in her old age. By the time she died, she had fifteen grandchildren and forty-four great-grandchildren. She witnessed the change from horse and buggy to motor car. Also the rise of industry, creation of airplanes and hundreds of other wonderful inventions, like electricity, telephones and indoor plumbing.

Two hundred people from the church turned out for Missy's funeral. She had dedicated a good portion of her spare time to helping others, showing them what the mercy of God's love could do in their lives. She spoke at women's meetings, and even visited hospitals, teaching women about the way Jesus had changed her life.

Luke, now seventy-one himself, knelt down beside her casket. "Grandfather, I know you're happy now. Mama is up there with you, keeping you and Margaret company. Thank you for praying for her, for never giving up. She turned her life around and affected so many people. I'm proud of her, all of us are. I praise you, Lord, for the mercy you've shown our family. Please let them all know I'll see them soon. Amen."

More from Energion Publications

Personal Study

The Character of Our Discontent	$12.99
The Jesus Paradigm	$17.99
Finding My Way in Christianity	$16.99
When People Speak for God	$17.99
Not Ashamed of the Gospel	$12.99
What's In A Version?	$12.99
The Messiah and His Kingdom to Come	$19.99 (B&W)

Christian Living

The Sacred Journey	$12.99
Daily Devotions of Ordinary People – Extraordinary God	$19.99
Directed Paths	$7.99
Grief: Finding the Candle of Light	$8.99
I Want to Pray	$7.99
Soup Kitchen for the Soul	$12.99
Victim No More!	$12.99

Bible Study

From Inspiration to Understanding	$24.99
Learning and Living Scripture	$12.99
Philippians: A Participatory Study Guide	$9.99
Ephesians: A Participatory Study Guide	$9.99
To the Hebrews: A Participatory Study Guide	$9.99
Revelation: A Participatory Study Guide	$9.99
The Gospel According to St. Luke: A Participatory Study Guide	$8.99
Identifying Your Gifts and Service: Small Group Edition	$12.99
Why Four Gospels?	$11.99

Theology

God's Desire for the Nations	$18.99
Operation Olive Branch	$16.99
Christian Archy	$9.99
Ultimate Allegiance	$9.99
The Politics of Witness	$9.99

Fiction

Megabelt	$12.99

www.ingramcontent.com/pod-product-compliance
Lightning Source LLC
LaVergne TN
LVHW051012080826
845145LV00009B/2588
* 9 7 8 1 8 9 3 7 2 9 1 4 8 *